DISINFECT THIS!

Stupidity, Hypocrisy and Lies in a Pandemic on The Road to the 2020 Presidential Election

JASON VINES
Cover by Henry Payne

Table Of Contents

INTRODUCTION 7

CHAPTER ONE

**"I SCREAM, YOU SCREAM,
WE ALL SCREAM FOR ICE CREAM!"** 13

Bad News For Democrats: The End May
(Or May Not) Be Near 14

"A Day In The Life" Of Nancy Pelosi... 17

The Real "Strategy" And "Vision" Of Porky Pig Pelosi................ 19

"Unite The Country?" I Thought You Said "Ignite!"................... 23

CHAPTER TWO

"BAD TRUMP HUNTING" 26

Everyone Is A Hero Compared To Trump 27

Trump, The French And The Newest Hoax:
Trump Is A "Snake Oil" Salesman 30

Dr. Fauci: The Trump-Hating Left Wants You!........................... 33

Trump Isn't Firing Dr. Fauci, And The Left Goes Bat Crazy 35

Surprise! Surprise! Surprise! Wapo Has A Beef With Trump 36

Class In Session Online: Deductive Reasoning
Regarding The Virus 37

Disinfecting The "World-Is-Ending"
Over Trump's "Musings" 39

Channeling Rahm: Never Let A Distraction
"Waste" A Crisis 42

Obama Gets Tacky, Typically Divisive
As Cnn Fails Journalism 101 47

Cuomo Accepts Blame For Elderly Deaths…
Ah, Not! 51

New York Times And Dems Have Paranoid
Panties In A Bunch 54

Biden Is Rubber, Trump Is Glue 57

CHAPTER THREE

DEMOCRATS GONE WILD! 60

The Good, Bad And The Ugly During
The Virus Crisis…So Far 61

Again, Why I Love This Country 64

I Love To Count!!!!! 65

Just As We Suspected, The Corona Virus Is Racist 67

The First Democratic National Committee
Meeting Now That Bernie Is Toast
Satire 68

Dumbest Famous Human On Earth Identified
Satire 72

Wow! A New Low -- Impeaching Trump
For Taking On Corruption! 74

Mia During The Coronavirus Crisis: The U.s. Congress 76

Cuomo: Don't Let My People Go! 78

Fly Little Jail Birdy, Fly, Fly Away 80

Democratic Oversight Of The Coronavirus Money?
Heck, Let's Get Former Detroit Mayor Kwame Kilpatrick Out
Of The Hoosegow And Put Him In Charge Of "Oversight" 82

A Huge Taxpayer Bailout Of Illinois?
It's Music To The Dems' Ears 84

Get A Clue: November Presidential Election Will Happen 88

Defying Charitable Work To Save Lives In The Coronavirus Crisis, Gay Nyc
Councilman Proves He's A Bigoted Horse's Ass 90

Russian Collusion Hoax Revealed: Finally,
And Heads Will Roll 91

CHAPTER FOUR

THE SMITTEN MITTEN 94

Michigan Guv Gretchen Whitmer: Sometimes You Feel Like A Nut........... 95

Guv Whitmer Declares Abortion
A "Life-Sustaining" Necessity In Tough Times 97

Michigan Democratic State Legislators
"Disinfect" The Germ In Their Midst 99

Essentially Determining "Essential Workers"
According To Michigan Guv Almond Joy... 101

Guv Whitmer: Metoo Backs Biden;
No Garden Seeds For You, Maybe Forever! 104

Michigan Be Dammed! Trump Persona Non Grata............................... 106

Michigan Boatgate: Guv Whitmer Is Rudderless!
Part Two: The Grand Illusion... 110

Convict Kwame Kilpatrick "Ain't To Proud To Bail" 114

CHAPTER FIVE

SOME CONSERVATIVES GO FULL STUPID 117

A Message To The Few, The Proud, The Stupid In Michigan 118

North Of The Southern Border: A Mexican Standoff In Michigan!.......... 119

CHAPTER SIX

AS SEEN, BUT NOT TO BE BELIEVED, ON T.V. AND THE INTERNET 121

Cnn's Chris Cuomo: Fake At Last! Fake At Last!
Thank God Almighty He Is Fake At Last! 122

Larry King Lies?.. 124

Google, Youtube And Free Speech: Another One Bites The Dust!............ 126

Cnn Intimates Trump Lying About Seeing Coronavirus
Origins Evidence And Lacks Basic Reading Skills............................ 129

Jimmy Kimmel: The Lyin' King 131

Censorship And A Biased Media:
The Hits Just Keep On A Comin'! 132

Liberal Censorship On Steroids.. 135

Update! Update! Read All About It! Clapper Lies Again! 137

Lying Is Easy When The Interviewer Is Coaching You 138

Move Over Carrot Top; We've Got "Aimless" And Andy.................. 139

No Voter Fraud? Check Your "Facts" Fact Checkers!........................ 141

Chris Cuomo: "I've Fallen And I Can't Get Up!" 144

CHAPTER SEVEN

JOSEPH BIDEN
AND THE TECHNICOLOR FINGER PUPPET 147

Biden Calls Michigan Guv Whitmer: It Wasn't Pretty
Satire.. 148

Biden Gets Major Endorsement He Can't Fathom
Satire.. 150

Joe Biden: His Finger On The Pulse Of, Um, Er, Nevermind
Satire.. 152

Hillary Gets Behind Joe Biden: Thank God! She Is Safe There! 154

Obama To Biden: I'm Gonna Keep On Loving You! 155

#Believewomen #Believejoebiden
#Believewhatever #Ripleysbelieveordont 158

Joe, Hunter And An Atm.. 160

Biden And Obama: The Unmasked Singers
Satire.. 162

Biden And Warren "Pow Wow" For Campaign Video
Satire.. 166

Joe Biden: In "God's Name" 171

CHAPTER EIGHT

MY LITTLE CHINA GIRL 173

For Immmediate Release No Tickee, No Virus Satire 174

Kim Jong, Uh, Jung, Uh, Un, Wtf, Is Dead! Maybe Satire 175

Commie Toiret Papel Finarry Allives – Mega Pack! 176

CHAPTER NINE

"THE FINALE" 178

A Crises Collision And A Sick "Fear" It Will Go Away 179

A Den Of Liberal Photo Thieves 182

EPILOGUE 185
ACKNOWLEDGMENTS 187
ABOUT THE AUTHOR 189

INTRODUCTION

"WE HAVE TO DESTROY THE VILLAGE TO SAVE IT!"

Although it began in earnest in late January, I didn't start writing on Facebook every day or so about the growing Coronavirus or COVID-19 pandemic until early March. By the beginning of April, I had seen quite enough of the biased reporting, garbage predictions and "holier-than-thou" pontificating regarding the deadly virus – the seemingly hourly barrage of stupidity, hypocrisy and lies surrounding the pandemic.

I came to the conclusion that it all had very little to do with people getting infected and, sadly, thousands dying. But it had everything to do with the 2020 General Election in November where we decide most importantly the next President of the United States, and secondarily which party will lead both or either the U.S. House of Representatives and the U.S. Senate.

Fueling this crisis, beyond the sick and dying, was the fact that our economy was cratering as businesses – big and small -- were locked down, tens of millions of Americans lost their jobs and people were asked to stay home except for emergencies. Some of those "stay home" directives were "suggestions," while others were enforced resembling the closest thing we have had to martial law in our lifetime, especially in the Democrat-controlled states of New York, Michigan and California.

I made it my mission to call out the perpetrators of the stupidity, hypocrisy and lies daily, sometimes many times during the day on my Facebook page. My posts started to gain a loyal following: mostly conservatives like me, but also liberal FB friends – some willing to engage in healthy, adult banter, but most just lobbing F-bombs and other profanity and casting dispersions on me and my fellow conservatives. I think I have been called a racist, homophobe, xenophobe, misogynist – you name it – more in the last two months than I have in my entire life. Few if any of the liberals berating me ever countered the facts I had laid out. And, of course, I was berated constantly for supporting the policies of our President, Donald Trump, otherwise known as The Orangeman.

So, I started to write and post and the positive feedback I received and the number of times my FB friends "shared" my posts, kept me going and going. Oh, the negative, usually profane and mean responses from the liberals DID NOT slow me down. Actually, they inspired me as much or more than the positive responses. If that sounds weird, it really isn't. It's actually par for the course, even though so many states banned golf during the height of the pandemic.

I learned years ago that if you are an opinion writer and all you get is "positive" feedback, you are not doing your job. I got that bit of intelligence from the chief editorial writer at the **Detroit News**, Nolan Finley. While we were both contributors to the **Detroit News'** conservative political website, "**The Michigan View,**" created by my friend, political cartoonist Henry Payne, I asked Nolan if the negative comments on his opinion pieces ever got to him. He answered with an emphatic "No" and shared his knowledge about how the game is played.

For **The Michigan View**, Henry Payne asked me to contribute what I love best – satire. My political satire over the next four years was some of the most fun I have had in my life. And I was paid richly for it – nothing. And it was worth it to me. In 2015, at Henry's suggestion, I compiled my columns in my second book, **"Jimmy Hoffa Called My Mom a Bitch: Profiles in Stupidity."**

The title was a reference to one of my better columns compiled in the book. On Labor Day 2011, James P. Hoffa, Jr., President of the Teamsters' Union and son of the infamous Jimmy Hoffa, was joined by President Barack Obama on a stage in downtown Detroit to celebrate the holiday with thousands of union members from the Teamsters, the UAW and others. It was really not a "celebration," but rather a day to verbally smack around Republicans.

Jimmy was the emcee and spent his time crucifying his Republican enemies until he announced his battle cry:

"We got to keep an eye on the battle that we face. The war on workers. And you see it everywhere, it is the Tea Party. And you know, there is only one way to beat and win this war. The one thing about working people is we like a good fight. And you know what? They've got a war; they've got a war with us and there's only going to be one winner. It's going to be the workers of Michigan, and America. We're going to win that war."

Turning to President Obama on the stage, Hoffa channeled Spartacus (my apologies to Senator Cory Booker, ahem) and screamed, "President Obama, this is your army. We are ready to march. LET'S TAKE THESE SONS OF BITCHES OUT AND GIVE AMERICA BACK TO AMERICA WHERE WE BELONG!"

Sure, it was poor sentence structure, but that is not what got to me. As I thought about his speech, I suddenly realized that Jimmy Hoffa Jr. was talking about ME. I was one of the sonofabitches he wanted to "take out." And then it hit me: if I was a sonofabitch, then Jimmy Hoffa had just called my mom a BITCH!

The great news about this book is that I had more than enough stupidity, hypocrisy and lies to choose from over the sixty-one days between April 1 to May 31, 2020 in which these columns incapsulate. The more I wrote, the more feedback I got from my FB friends and many began encouraging me to not only keep going, but to put my columns, my posts, in a book. And then one magical day, I received a reply to a post from a particularly nasty Liberal FB friend telling me to "get a job."

Well, here it is.

The title of the book, ***"Disinfect This!"*** was inspired by my column "Disinfecting the World-is-Ending Over Trump's 'Musings'" in the "Bad Trump Hunting" chapter of the book. You may recall that in one press briefing on April 24th with his Virus Task Force, the President asked the doctors on the stage if there was any possibility that a "disinfect" could be developed to "inject" into the human body and kill the Coronavirus. As one news organization put it, Trump was "musing." The rest of the MSM went bonkers and reported that Trump had TOLD, or at least suggested, that Americans inject themselves with Lysol or Clorox.

In that column, I said that Trump's "musing" was stupid, but only for one reason: knowing the Trump-hating liberal media would claim that the mad Orangeman was TELLING Americans to inject NOW, which the MSM dutifully did. Hysteria, sort of, ensued and the media waited with bated breath for someone, anyone to actually inject a disinfect on "Trump's orders" and buy the farm. It didn't happen as I believe even the dumbest Americans are not that dumb. Darwinism did not rear its ugly head. OK, some moron in Arizona drank some pool or aquarium chemical that sounded somewhat like the infamous Hydro Chloroquine and kicked the bucket, but that was before Trump's "musing."

One reply to that column on Facebook was from a dear friend who is Liberal to the core. "Why are you defending Trump?" she asked. Well, I wasn't defending Trump. I called him stupid. But, the purpose of the column was to show, yet again, how biased our Trump-hating MSM is, to the point that they would attempt to create hysteria by misrepresenting what the President actually said.

If you like the book, and it helps you remember the stupidity, hypocrisy and lies we witnessed during the Coronavirus pandemic, share it or better yet tell your friends to buy it. If you don't and agree with Hillary Clinton that "WHAT DIFFERENCE, AT THIS POINT, DOES

IT MAKE!", well, keep it in the bathroom. You never know when toilet paper will get scarce again and it might come in, well, handy.

CHAPTER ONE

"I SCREAM, YOU SCREAM,

WE ALL SCREAM FOR ICE CREAM!"

BAD NEWS FOR DEMOCRATS: THE END MAY (OR MAY NOT) BE NEAR

WARNING: SATIRE. DO NOT READ WHILE INJECTING LYSOL, CLOROX or POOL CLEANING CHEMICALS! DO NOT READ WHILE CLEANING YOUR AR-15 "FULLY AUTOMATIC" WEAPON!

Minutes ago, my totally unreliable sources, emailed me a bootleg copy of a phone conversation earlier this morning between DNC Chairman Tom Perez and Democratic House Speaker Nancy Pelosi. While I cannot verify the authenticity of the phone conversation, I am following current MSM protocol and am sharing it with you regardless of whether it is true or fake.

PEREZ: Good morning Madam Speaker, I have some good news and some bad news. Which do you want first?

PELOSI: If the "good news" involves the words "Trump" and "a massive stroke" or "stock market crashes" or "unemployment hits 20 percent" or "the White House stupidly won't let Dr. Fauci testify," I'll take that first.

PEREZ: Unfortunately, the "good news" isn't that good, but it ain't bad.

PELOSI: OK, what is it?

PEREZ: The secretary of the U.S. Senate says it cannot release any documents regarding Joe Biden's tenure in the chamber, so we won't see any ugly Tara Reade memos.

PELOSI: Tom, as a woman, I find that offensive; Tara Reade is not "that" ugly.

PEREZ: No, no, no. I meant "ugly" as in ugly things about Joe Biden and this lying woman who claims he let his fingers do the walking, if you know what I mean.

PELOSI: But, about Joe's records stored at the University of Delaware?

PEREZ: Well, Joe has said there is NOTHING to see in any of the stored documents there. And, as we have solemnly and prayerfully determined, "he must be believed."

PELOSI: Yep, that's good enough for me, hashtag "Believe Joe" – hee, hee, hee. OK, what's the bad news. NO WAIT! Hold on a second. I need to get a couple of scoops of ice cream before I hear the bad news. (Delay) OK, go for it. I am prepared. Rocky Road always takes the edge off of bad news. Mmm!

PEREZ: OK, get ahold of yourself as this may be hard to take.

PELOSI: I can, OH CRAP, I'm getting a brain freeze!!! Alright, there, whew, go ahead.

PEREZ: The COVID-19, or as Joe Biden calls it, COVID-9, DEATHS in the U.S. have fallen for five consecutive days, with some of the biggest decreases in both deaths and hospitalizations in New York City. We may be on the verge of losing our greatest weapon against the Orangeman.

PELOSI: Damn that Cuomo and Mayor Big Bird!!!!! We had a plan!

PEREZ: I know, I know. I mean, you gotta give those guys a little bit of credit for forcing all those elderly folks with the virus back into their retirement facilities to infect others.

PELOSI: So, why the hell isn't it working anymore, dammit?

PEREZ: Um, they all died. We've got no more "fuel" in the tank. But there is a "silver lining," no pun intended.

PELOSI: What? Are we going to bring in a s—tload of elderly illegal aliens from Central America and throw them in virus-infected old folk's homes?

PEREZ: Damn, how did you know?

PELOSI: Zeke Emmanuel sent me a text an hour ago. I guess it was his idea. He said if we don't do this, the deaths will continue to fall, states will open up and our economy will recover, maybe even before the November election – the very definition of Armageddon. Zeke thinks his plan will keep this pandemic going for at least 18 months. It's messy, but desperate times call for desperate measures. And, lots of ice cream. But I want NONE of those Central American old bastards in my San Francisco. With my luck, they'll slip on a pile of vagrant poop on the sidewalk and die and we won't be able to blame it on the Coronavirus.

PEREZ: Good thinking, Madam Secretary. How's that ice cream?

PELOSI: Gone, dammit! Ah well, back to the kitchen!

"A DAY IN THE LIFE" OF NANCY PELOSI

Yesterday, Democratic House Speaker Nancy Pelosi dropped an 1,800-plus page, $3 trillion "stimulus" package which she plans to discuss on the House floor May 15th. In announcing the "Heroes Act," as Pelosi calls it, Senate Republicans have already deemed it "dead on arrival." That is exactly what Pelosi and the Democrats are hoping for: this is not about virus crisis relief as much as it is about a 2020 campaign issue to kill those heartless, mean and, of course, racist Republicans led by the Orangeman.

Pelosi did somewhat blow it in announcing the package by inserting ONE unnecessary word in her pronouncement: ONLY. She said the $3 trillion package is "ONLY centered" on the impact of the pandemic. When something is "centered" there is no need for the word "only." First is first. Last is last. And, centered is centered. Period.

But the "only" line will be ripped apart when the bill is fully explored. Early reads show the "Heroes Act" is filled with pork to please a progressive "wish list" and curry favor with their constituents. There are billions for illegal immigrants in the bill. There is a provision to allow federal tax deductions of state and local taxes which benefits most the wealthy liberals in those states with high taxes – New York, New Jersey, California and Illinois. It proposes to empty much of the prison population and put them back on the streets. The bill mentions – 68 times -- aid for cannabis and marijuana purveyors, especially in urban areas of our country. Finally, there is about $500 billion for state coffers. Were state governments impacted negatively by the virus crisis? Of course. But much of the proposed money would be used to bailout financial malfeasance long before COVID-19 hit our shores, especially in New York, Illinois and California.

It makes me want to cry. But why cry when you can sing?

My apologies to Lennon and McCartney, or is it Lenin and FDR
I read the news today, oh boy
About a gal who made a "virus" taxpayer raid
And though the news was rather sad
Well, I just had to laugh
I saw the early draft

She blew her mind out with a scoop
She didn't see the ice cream's temp had changed
A crowd of Americans stood and stared
They'd seen brain freeze before
Nobody was really sure if she was from the House of Wax

I saw a video today, oh boy
It had been edited by NBC
A crowd of Liberals thought it real
But I just couldn't watch
Knowing it was a crock
I'd love to turn it off

Woke up, Nanc' fell out of bed
Dragged some dye across her head
Found her way downstairs, had a waffle cone
And looking up, she noticed she was late
Found her Botox and grabbed some pearls
Made the Limo in a second's whirl
Found her way upstairs and had a scoop

A staffer spoke and brought her more ice cream

I read the news today, oh boy
Three trillion dollars in pork-laden stimulus
Though legit virus relief rather small
They had to tout it all
Now they know the pork it takes to fill the Congressional hall
I'd love to stim-u-late you on

THE REAL "STRATEGY" AND "VISION" OF PORKY PIG PELOSI

As a Democrat, you know you kind of blew it when liberal stalwart *The New York Times* doesn't take your "vision" hook, line and sinker. Remember that word "vision."

Last night, the U.S. House of Representative narrowly passed Speaker Nancy Pelosi's "Heroes Act," the Dems' answer to saving Americans from the Coronavirus crisis and on the heels of the Republicans' two trillion-dollar relief package passed in April. It narrowly passed, 208 to 199, because some moderate Democrats from their more-conservative districts knew they could not sell this pork-laden bill with a straight face to their voters back home.

From my home state of Iowa, Congresswoman Cindy Axne rejected the "bloated" bill because she "could not in good conscience vote to accept this Washington gamesmanship, or vote to approve unrelated wastes of taxpayer dollars". You go, Iowa girl! She didn't use the word "pork" because in Iowa, pork is not a dirty word. Nor should it be anywhere in our great land, outside of Washington D.C. because pork equals God's gift to mankind: bacon.

Of course, the Iowa Congresswoman will be shunned by Nancy Pelosi and possibly "Axned" to grovel to get back in the Speaker's good graces.

Pelosi was at her sanctimonious and hypocritical best arguing on the House floor for members to drink her "Big Fat Sow" of a bill. (My apologies to Steely Dan.) "It's always interesting to me to see how much patience some people have with the pain and suffering of other people," she said.

Patience? Does she mean like "patiently" standing in front of a $24K freezer and gorging on $14 a pint ice cream while food lines stretch from L.A. to NYC and grocery stores struggle to keep up with the demand for toilet paper, paper towels, disinfecting wipes and some food products? Does she mean like "patiently" delaying the original rescue bill for a week while people struggled to pay their bills and small businesses tittered on the brink of bankruptcy? Her tone deafness is obviously a negative side effect of Botox and Poligrip.

As she argued on the floor of the House yesterday, Pelosi tried to hide her true intentions in one sentence that I am sure she thought would be remembered throughout history, despite being complete B.S. "This is a very strategically planned piece of legislation that is tailored strictly to meet the needs of the American people regarding the coronavirus pandemic, she said."

"Tailored strictly" to take on the needs of the American people in the virus crisis? Hardly. Arts endowments, financial aid for marijuana purveyors and a bailout of D.C.-based lobbying firms is hardly part of a "strictly tailored" bill relating to Coronavirus suffering.

But in that sentence is her real goal, and that of the Democrats, as they use this terrible crisis to change our country. She said this bill was a "strategically planned piece of legislation."

It's "strategically planned" to make Republicans (read: Trump) look heartless and cruel, and watch, ultimately racist, while knowing there is no way in hell this beast could ever pass. Her bill is called the "Heroes Act," but it should be called the "Divide and Conquer Act." You can't blame her. She learned it from the master, her Sensei: former President Obama.

Here's the line from *The New York Times* coverage of the bill that made me realize that even The Gray Lady wasn't buying what Pelosi was selling: "Even though the bill was more a messaging document than a viable piece of legislation, its fate was in doubt in the final hours before its passage."

Even the *Times* could see through Nancy's bluster about helping the "American people." It's all about the November election and has nothing to do with helping Americans NOW or she would have crafted a bill that would pass in a non-partisan fashion.

Only one Republican, Peter King of New York, supported the bill, while 14 Democrats opposed their own party's bill. I really don't blame King. I like him, and for the most part he has supported this Administration, and his state has been hit harder than any other. He knew it would pass, so in the end, his vote was inconsequential, and he gets to tell his constituents that he was looking out for them when this turd gets flushed in the Senate.

The "Heroes Act" contains a number of "strictly tailored" Coronavirus priorities, including $100 billion for rental assistance and $75 billion in mortgage relief. But then the pig gets out of the pen with $3.6 billion for "election security" and a $25 billion bailout for the Postal Service. I am certain that Americans sitting around the kitchen table, trying to figure out how to pay the bills without a job, are saying, "But honey, what I am most interested in this time of turmoil is election security." "Yes, sweetheart, I can't sleep at night thinking about it."

The bill would also temporarily suspend the limit on the deduction of state and local taxes from Federal income taxes. Oh, that sounds great as most working Americans pay those. But, and here's Nancy's strategy, it would disproportionately benefit wealthy taxpayers in ridiculously high-tax states like New York, New Jersey, Illinois and California. The rich folks in those states are key to filling the Democratic campaign coffers.

The leftist of the Lefties in the Dem party was none too happy with the bill for one reason or another, including not doing enough to enrich illegal aliens. But, for the most part, they held their noses (a good thing with pork in your midst) and voted it up. But then, there was Congresswoman Pramila Jayapal of the state of Washington, who voted no.

Jayapal committed a mortal political sin in April when she admitted that she and her progressive colleagues had been blocking legislation aimed at providing relief to small business workers in order to "hold on to political leverage." Now, most of the Dems agree with her, but you are not supposed to "voice it." It is OK to have it as part of your "core inner monologue" as a Liberal, but you don't shout it out.

Yesterday on the House floor, Jayapal couldn't help herself. "This is a crisis. People are really trying to figure out what they want to do, and I just want to respect that," she said. "But this is supposed to be our vision."

There. That word. Vision. It's not about helping Americans NOW; it's all about how the Democrats see this country going forward, THEIR country, say, after what they hope is a joyous November.

"UNITE THE COUNTRY?" I THOUGHT YOU SAID "IGNITE!"

Enjoying my coffee early this morning and preparing for a cooler-than-normal day in the Arizona desert, I saw a rare thing in our highly partisan environment. It was a campaign ad for Joe Biden created by the folks at Unite the Country PAC. It shows Joe as a kid, how his father sacrificed for the family and how Joe as Vice President was, at least on the video, the major savior of the auto industry and much of the American economy in the dire days of The Great Recession. It ended with the theme: BIDEN – Unite the Country.

Throwing off my partisan overcoat, I thought it was pretty swell. Moments later, I read a story on Google where Biden has nicknamed Donald Trump "President Tweety." I didn't "thought I saw a putty cat," rather I just rolled my eyes. Why? Simple. I guess 'ol Joe had learned nothing from the 2016 presidential campaign where "Little Marco" Rubio tried to "out-Trump" Trump and it killed his campaign. Joe, trust me, you cannot pull this off so stop trying.

Back to the "Unite the Country" campaign ad for Biden. I admit it is a noble cause, however, it appears that some (I believe most) of Biden's "civil" Democratic supporters want no part of it.

Two cases in point.

The first happened this morning on ABC's Trump-hating *"The View."* One of the ladies anchoring the show, Sunny Hostin, claimed that the evil Orangeman and his ever-cruel, heartless and racist Republican minions in Congress were balking at the latest coronavirus relief bill because they didn't want "the have-nots to survive this."

For Hostin there was absolutely no other reason that made sense for Republicans to hold back on the pork-laden $3 trillion Nancy Pelosi "Heroes Act" that passed the House largely along party lines last week. In her mind, those Republican Congresspeople and President Trump wanted one thing and one thing only from this Coronavirus: Dead poor people, knowing a disproportionate share of those "have-nots" are people of color, like her.

Co-host Megan McCain tried to counter Hostin's "victimhood" spiel, saying that the Pelosi bill wasn't supported by most Republicans because it included a number of billions-of-dollars provisions that had nothing to do with coronavirus. "That is just ridiculous. It's a Democrat wish list. It's ridiculous," she said.

Hostin is not alone in ignoring the new, positive "Unite the Country" theme of the Biden campaign.

Yesterday, President Trump acknowledged that he had been given Hydro Chloroquine, along with zinc, to keep him healthy amid the virus crisis. The media of course went nutso and sought out every "expert" they could find that would say the drug cocktail doesn't work and could cause harm. Senator Chuck Schumer called Trump's announcement "reckless." Of course, throughout the day I heard one "expert" criticize the drug, followed by another "expert" that said there is evidence that it has worked.

But comparatively to House Speaker Nancy Pelosi, Schumer was hitting Trump with small jabs. Pelosi decided to go "full ugly" and declared that Trump should not be using Hydro Chloroquine because he is "morbidly obese." Not a bit chunky. Not a few pounds over the legal limit and not standard-fare obese, but morbidly obese.

Hey Nancy, if you want to see morbid obesity, put your "Heroes Act" up to the mirror. Its morbid obesity is the very reason it will die quickly in the U.S. Senate and the "have-nots" that Sunny Hostin says

Republicans want to kill will "have nothing" from the "Divide and Conquer" game you thought you could play for one reason: winning the 2020 General Election.

So much for "Uniting the Country," ladies.

CHAPTER TWO

"BAD TRUMP HUNTING"

EVERYONE IS A HERO COMPARED TO TRUMP

The Trump Haters are beside themselves, despite their hypocritical calls for "unity." The latest example involves Queen Elizabeth. More on that later.

Of course, the Left has been calling for Trump's demise even before he was inaugurated in January 2017. Congressthings Al Green and Maxine Waters called for his impeachment before he took residence on Pennsylvania Avenue. Earlier this year, the Trump Haters succeeded in actually impeaching him over a phone call with the Ukraine, which, funny, ended up only hurting Uncle Joe Biden thanks to the former VP's crackhead, multimillionaire-out-of-thin-air son.

Like Russia, Russia, Russia, the Ukraine phoner was overplayed by the Trump Haters and he actually came out stronger. What to do, what to do. Hmmm. Ah, a global pandemic! Yeah, that's the ticket! As Flounder said in Animal House, "This is going to be great!"

The charges began quickly. Trump was slow to react. Ah, he, among world leaders, stopped travel from China first, along with Italy. Oh, yeah, right, right, North Korea's Kim did it two days earlier, but then, how many flights go into North Korea on a daily basis. As I have dutifully pointed out previously, Dick-Tater Kim, a pure genius and humanitarian, reports "ZERO" cases of Covid-19 in his country. My unreliable sources say that North Korea is rife with Covid-17 and Covid-20, just no Covid-19. Yesterday, Kim told the Unassociated Press that he "brames evewything on my buddy, Tlump."

Trump is doing nothing; it is all the state governors! Well, well, it is apparent that the Trump-led Federal government is moving mountains to cut red tape and regulations to support the states, and have done so since Day One, or Day less-than-one. NY Guv Andrew Cuomo early-on tried to bitch-slap the Prez, until he realized he had two skeletons in the closet: he had 4,000 unused ventilators ready for active duty, gathering dust in a warehouse across the Hudson River and, in 2015, he had hundreds of millions of dollars set aside to buy medical equipment in advance, and he opted to use it for a solar panel company that went belly-up in a NY minute.

Cuomo, who's no dummy (and loving the daily spotlight where he could talk about his Mama's meatballs), realized where his baguette was buttered and played nice with the Trump Administration as he received, literally, a boatload of help – a real Navy hospital ship and temporary hospitals thanks to Trump, FEMA and the Army Corp of Engineers at Javits Center and temporary hospitals (think MASH units) in Central Park thanks to Samaritan's Purse, Franklin Graham's Christian relief organization. Oh, my, those silly, silly Christians.

Same goes for another hero-other-than-Trump, California Guv Gavin Newsom, who has brawled with Trump for years, but put aside his Trump Hate, and worked with the President and the Federal agencies, to help his people. Good on you, Gavin.

Not so much for the Michigan governor, as Trump called, "that woman." Yes, bad form on Trump's part, for sure, but remember that she "dude-slapped" Trump from the get-go, and only kind of toned it down when Trump hit back. Of course, in the MSM, Trump was attacking her even though SHE, that woman, ahem, threw the first punch. Typical.

The good news for Michigan Guv Whitmer, she's on the list to be Uncle Joe's running mate as he categorically said he is picking "a woman." Not the best running mate, not the most qualified, simply based on gender. Geez, I hope Whitmer is "IDENTIFYING" as a woman in the fall, or Joe has pooped the bed again.

OK, finally to the Queen. She is such a great leader – compared to Trump – in these dire times. But first, let's get into the Way-Back Machine to November 30, 2018. Sadly, on that day, a hero of mine, former President George H.W. Bush, died. He was truly a hero, in war and in government. But the media HATED him when he was in office, ridiculing him non-stop, every day. Dana Carvey made bank on him on SNL.

But, when he bought the farm, he was great according to the most-hating media, ah, compared to President Donald J. Trump. The MSM put Bush on a pedestal for one and only one reason: to skewer Trump. What a bunch of phonies.

Which brings us to today, or, yesterday. Queen Elizabeth gave an inspiring speech about unifying Great Britain during this crisis. It was, as the Brits say, spot on. It reminded me of her father's speech decades earlier during WWII. The media and the Left, sorry about the redundancy, jumped on it and questioned, "Why can't our President be like this?"

Well, Queen Liz is NOT in charge of directing Federal agencies to act. Liz is NOT working actively with large, medium and small businesses to change their businesses and provide much needed medical equipment overnight. No, Liz spends her days poking voodoo dolls of Camilla (Chuck's wife) and Meghan Markle (Harry's wife).

Queen Liz is not working with the banks to provide financial relief to small businesses, the engine of our economy. Liz is not directing her tax agency to cut sustaining checks to families across her land. No, the Queen is, proudly, offering support and hope. A good and proper thing to do, but then, as they say, hope is not a strategy.

I doubt Trump has crumpets and tea after his press conferences, now not broadcasted by bitter MSNBC and CNN (this will change) while those networks view Guv Cuomo's pressers as Must-See TV.

For my Liberal friends who will hate me even further for this

Facebook post, please, please, list Trump's actual mistakes and IMPORTANTLY what YOU, as pandemic experts, would do differently. And please, stop posting about how the country should unify and in the next post, slam our President. I know, I know, it is what you have been doing, daily, since November 2016. But please, give it a rest unless you have better answers.

Be a little less Maxine Waters, and a bit more like Queen Liz.

TRUMP, THE FRENCH AND THE NEWEST HOAX: TRUMP IS A "SNAKE OIL" SALESMAN

Yesterday on *MarketWatch*, author Steve Goldstein debunked the media's newest anti-Trump obsession – that the President was hyping "unproven" Hydro Chloroquine as a drug for use in fighting Coronavirus BECAUSE he has a stake in one of the companies that is making the drug that could enrich him. Of course, the French company has been making this drug for about 50 years in the fight against malaria and Lupus.

This newest hoax comes at the same time that many MSM outlets are begrudgingly backtracking on their claims that the drug is a fraudulent "snake oil" after more and more reports that the drug is indeed working. Just ask the Democratic state representative in Detroit, Michigan, who recovered quickly from "near death" from Coronavirus after taking the drug, as well as news reports that almost 100 percent of doctors in The Bronx, hard hit by the virus, are using the drug for their patients and themselves.

The latest hoax, with little if any proof, began as a "theory" by the "Trump-loving" *The New York Times*, quickly parroted by *The*

Huffington Post, and then turbocharged by Mika Brzezinski on the Trump-hating "***Morning Joke***" on MSNBC. Throughout the day, several of my liberal FB friends perpetuated this hoax, again with no proof – just lemmings falling over the cliff in an effort to cast dispersions on Trump as they have been for going on four years.

Yeah, that's the ticket! Trump doesn't care about those suffering; he only wants to get even richer! Again, the MSM is beginning to show egg on their faces for their previous claims that Trump was a snake oil salesman "pimping" for drug makers when he wasn't busy getting temporary hospitals built in days and having his Vice President coordinate a slew on unrelated businesses to turn over their manufacturing processes to make thousands of ventilators and millions of PPE masks.

The New York Times says Trump has a "small personal stake" in Sanofi, the French drug manufacturer that produces the drug. As Goldstein points out, "The report doesn't say how small, but it notes that his (Trump's) three family trusts have investments in a Dodge & Cox mutual fund whose largest holding is Sanofi. (I too have a fund with D&C and can't wait to be filthy rich.) A fund that matches this description is the Dodge & Cox International Stock Fund US:DODFX, which at last check was 3.3 percent invested in (the French drug maker) Sanofi."

So, the ***Times*** does not know the extent of the investment, yet can level a horrific charge against the President of the United States. Talk about sloppy, biased "journalism."

Then, Goldstein actually gets into the weeds (ah, he did his homework, unlike the Times) and found Trump's 2019 financial-disclosure form lists stakes in Family Trusts 1, 2 and 3 valued at between $1,001 and $15,000. (Whew, talk about a "wad o' cash, campers!) So according to Goldstein, "if Trump has the maximum $15,000 in each of the trusts, he holds a stake in Sanofi that's worth (at the maximum) $1,485

— and, at the minimum, just $99." Important note: the French drug maker does not sell the drug in the U.S.

Wow, Trump could soon be drowning in riches if he continues to push his "snake oil" and the reports keep getting better and better about the effectiveness of the drug. Sadly, I believe the MSM and the rest of the Left are wishing on a star that Hydro Chloroquine fails and Trump's "bigly" investment in the French drug maker goes belly-up, forcing Trump, his wife and son Baron to survive only on Kraft macaroni and cheese and powdered milk. Oh, the humanity!

Goldstein does suggest a fact unreported by the *Times*: "It turns out he (Trump) does look to have more than that modest sum invested in Sanofi, because, unmentioned in the Times report, his trusts also hold broader European stock market index funds." Again, if he holds more it is in a managed fund.

Goldstein further explains: "The iShares Core MSCI EAFE ETF US:IEFA has 0.67% of its holdings in Sanofi, and Sanofi is a 0.78% holding for the iShares MSCI EAFE ETF US:EFA, which is neither surprising nor notable, in that the French drug maker is so large." Wow, "point-six-seven percent"? Hardly the mother lode, and no one, including the Times, knows Trump's holdings in either fund, except of course the fund managers.

But that hasn't stopped the *Times*, **Huffington Post** and MSNBC from shouting fire in a crowded theater. Oh wait, they are all closed. My bad. What we do know is that each day, heck, each hour, we hear more and more promising news about the effectiveness of Hydro Chloroquine, especially when piggybacked with zinc.

If the success of the drug continues on its current positive trajectory, do you think the naysayers – very few of which are medical experts – will admit they were wrong? Don't bet the farm, or, your shares in a French drug maker.

DR. FAUCI: THE TRUMP-HATING LEFT WANTS YOU!

The latest ever-evolving anti-Trump attack from the Left is an oldie-but-a-goodie: Trump was slow on the switch in making this virus a "big deal." But this time it comes with a bit more intrigue, adding that Trump ignored his Virus Team's chief expert, Dr. Fauci, and is soon throwing the good doctor overboard.

The latter is a wet dream for the Left. Sure, sure, the Left and the MSM (sorry for the redundancy) have gone from being skeptical about Fauci as his overall ratings in the general public soared, to openly questioning him (along with Dr. Birx) of being a Trump lackey, to now putting him on a pedestal hoping beyond hope that Trump cans him and makes him both a martyr and the Left's new Poster Boy. Kind of reminds you of the Left's yo-yoing treatment of another hero-goat-back-to-hero figure, namely former FBI Director James Comey.

Let's go to the actual timeline, shall we? Trump formed his Coronavirus task force on January 28th and three days later put a clamp on travel from China to the U.S. (The U.S. and Italy were the first countries to do this, with the exception of North Korea, but then who flies to North Korea on a good day.)

At the time of both, Trump said he "hoped" everything would be OK here but was taking the matter seriously. After all, the information he had on hand included lies, yes lies, from the Chinese Government throughout the month of January, maybe as early as December. Exacerbating this lack of good information was a near-total cover-up, protecting China, by the World Health Organization, for which the U.S. is the organization's largest funder, by far pertaining to country support. The U.S. gives the WHO 43 per dollars per U.S. citizen, while China gives a buck fourteen cents.

If anyone asks you what a buck fourteen buys these days, respond it buys corruption from the world's major health organization. Sorry, I digress.

So, where does the Left's imminent Knight in Shining Armor come in? Dr. Anthony Fauci cautioned in a television interview January 21 that "while we should take it seriously," the virus was "not a major threat to the people of the United States, and this is not something that the citizens of the United States right now should be worried about." That was just one week before Trump formed his task force.

Oh, you argue, concerning how deadly this virus has become and considering how easy it became to transmit from human to human, a week is like a year! But, during that week, the U.S. received no good intel from China or the WHO. In fact, those two bad actors were still saying there was little if any evidence of human transferability.

Now, we painfully know different. But on January 21st and on January 28th, we did not know, again, thanks to the Chinese Government and the WHO.

Meanwhile, Dr. Fauci, once the man of the hour for his intellect and claiming stage presence, is the "Democrats' Great White Hope" to finally, finally, put a stake in the heart of Donald Trump. Stormy Daniels and Michael Avenatti failed. A sickening attempt to destroy the life of Trump's latest appointee to the Supreme Court failed. Russia, Russia, Russia failed. A phone call with Ukraine failed. Impeachment failed, miserably, and only emboldened Trump. Bogus stories by **The New York Times** and MSNBC's Mika Brzezinski alleging Trump was benefitting "bigly" financially by pushing Hydro Chloroquine failed. Calling that drug Trump's "snake oil" failed as success story after success story came to light.

TRUMP ISN'T FIRING DR. FAUCI, AND THE LEFT GOES BAT CRAZY

What a world, what a world. The MSM floated the idea, the hope, that The Donald, OUR President of the United States, would do hari-kari and fire the smart, little, infectious disease dude, Dr. Andy Fauci. It was the story all day. Liberal pundits and "journalists" in the MSM had a perpetual "woody" all day. (Sorry for the crudeness. OK, to be less "man-specific," some journos were, um, er, "moist." Better?)

Well, well, it didn't happen, and it ain't gonna happen. Trump is too smart to feed into the MSM-contrived firestorm. In fact, if he wanted to fire the tiny genius, he saw the early press reports and said, "Andy, you are safe for only one reason: I want to 'effe' these frauds."

Trump saw the early "news" reports and, I believe, put on a Santa suit, walking through the White House, shouting "Ho, ho, ho." It was Santa Trump knowing that the MSM had given him a present, wrapped in perfect bows that he could shove up their collective bung holes.

And, he did.

The MSM in today's press briefings were beside themselves, interrupting the President of the United States as if he was Mike Tyson coming out of jail after being charged with spousal abuse. The CNN correspondent, surprisingly not James Acosta this time, fully embarrassed herself. The network will probably give her a medal. She needs a pink slip, period.

ABC's John Karr looked like he had just lost his dog in the briefing. Trump slayed him with each stupid question Karr posed.

Trump's shining moment was talking about how he was earlier on a call with many state governors. He pointed out that many, if not all the members of the press in attendance at the briefing were, probably, secretly on that same call – in the D.C. offices of the Democratic state governors. Been there, done that.

Yet, these "reporters" could not point out one negative remark from the governors. Hmmm.

So now, alas, the task of bringing down the President of the United States rests on the shoulders of a loveable, affable expert on infectious diseases. Dr. Fauci, the weight of the world is NOT on your shoulders. The weight of the TDS-infused, desperate and rudderless Democratic Party and the MSM is. Buckle your seat belt and "enjoy the ride."

SURPRISE! SURPRISE! SURPRISE! WAPO HAS A BEEF WITH TRUMP

The "Trump-loving" *Washington Post*, a "newspaper" that for two weeks refused to cover the sexual assault charges recently against Democratic candidate Joe Biden, has yet another beef with the President. In what the paper termed "unprecedented", the U.S. government relief checks being sent to individuals and families – some 70 million of them – will include the signature of the President.

According to WaPo, adding the President's signature to these checks, a feat akin to landing an astronaut on Mars, ahem, COULD, I repeat COULD delay the checks arrivals for up to two days, according to senior IRS officials. NOTE: Senior IRS officials have never had anything but good things to say about Republicans. Ha!

It's funny, I don't remember *The Washington Post* having a scintilla of a problem with House Speaker Nancy Pelosi holding up the bill FOR A WEEK that created these relief checks. Pelosi, of course, dutifully used the delay in order to secure "vital and essential" funding for the Kennedy Center, PBS and the Smithsonian – oink, oink.

You gotta love the selective outrage and hypocrisy exhibited here. Ah well, I am getting used to it by now.

CLASS IN SESSION ONLINE: DEDUCTIVE REASONING REGARDING THE VIRUS

I have never performed a tutorial, nor, alas, know what a "tutorial" means, actually. Heck, back in junior high (the politically correct decided to call junior high "Middle School," so as not to offend, ah, hell, who?) I think we had "tutorials," but, sadly, I was in the restroom, poking zits.

Oh my, I am having flashbacks! So, sorry. Back to the online tutorial-whatever. Today's lesson is about DEDUCTIVE REASONING.

"Deductive reasoning, also deductive logic, is the process of reasoning from one or more statements (premises) to reach a logically certain conclusion. Deductive reasoning goes in the same direction as that of the conditionals, and links premises with conclusions. If all premises are true, the terms are clear, and the rules of deductive logic are followed, then the conclusion reached is necessarily true."

OK, that last paragraph, I just plain stole from Wikipedia. It is NOT plagiarism, dammit! (I called former VP Joe Biden, told him my story and my fears of plagiarism, he gave me a thumbs up, and then said, "Hey, buddy, who are you? Are you delivering my damned pizza?!!!")

OK, back to today's lesson: Deductive Reasoning.

I hope you can download the latest "Opinion" piece from Jennifer Rubin of ***The Washington Post,*** which I have attached, maybe. The "newspaper" has designated her as their "Conservative Opinion Writer." Well, if that is true, then I am a Brad Pitt look-alike. God bless America, I am one sexy bitch. Fact is, since 2016, this "conservative writer," Jennifer Rubin, has penned more than one hundred anti-Trump columns, conservatively. Pun intended. Anyway, in her latest column, Rubin notes, "Here is how many people Trump killed." Oh, she includes a chart, making her argument, ah, chart-like.

So, class, let's look at the deductive reasoning behind Ms. Rubin's conclusion. Please take notes, but NOT, on toilet paper, that is in short supply, for God's sake. First, we must deal ONLY with facts.

FACT ONE: It is apparent, more and more each day, that the Covid-19 virus, commonly known as Coronavirus after the Mexican beer distiller, now owned by Belgians, paying $50 million for the rights to the virus, BEGAN in Wuhan, China. Wuhan is a tiny suburb in S.E. China with six gazillion people.

FACT TWO: The virus was, after initial denials, quickly spread among the Wuhan population and then spread throughout the, ah, WORLD, thanks to Boeing and Airbus, and a small Chinese freighter smuggling elephant tusks to San Francisco and THE Ohio State University.

FACT THREE: The World Health Organization, WHO, funded "bigly" by the United States of America, with pennies from China, channeled Kevin Bacon in Animal House, begging us to "Remain Calm." They, the WHO, "confirmed" the Chinese Communist government's claim that the virus was not "transferrable" from human to human.

FACT FOUR: The virus spread quickly to the U.S., Italy, Spain and around the world. "Few" Chinese actually got the virus. Wink, wink, nod, nod, don't ya know."

FACT FIVE: Hundreds of thousands of deaths, worldwide. More than 10,000 in NY City alone. More than a thousand in Detroit.

So, with these facts, WHAT can we deduce, class???

I have an answer online from Timmy, a third grader, in Toledo, Ohio. Timmy says, "My mom and dad said it is Trump's fault."

Wow, the first answer, thanks to deductive reasoning, and Timmy's parents help, is CORRECT. "Thanks, Timmy! Tell your parents I said 'hi'."

Oh, Timmy is writing back: "I will tell them when they come back in the house. They're on the back-porch smoking medicine, they call it that, and eating Fritos and drinking a big jug of 'grape juice'."

God bless you, Tiny Tim.

DISINFECTING THE "WORLD-IS-ENDING" OVER TRUMP'S "MUSINGS"

Much more than usual traffic on my Facebook page and in emails, regarding President Trump's "suggestion" that we inject disinfectants into our bodies to kill the China, oops, Coronavirus, also known as Covid-19 by the medical establishment, and Covid-9 by Joe Biden.

To basically summarize the questions I am being asked, here goes: "Jason, try to defend (your) President regarding his call to inject yourself with disinfectant to kill the Coronavirus."

OK, quickly. President Trump's "musings" about an internal disinfectant were stupid – WAIT – considering the "gotcha now" mentally of the MSM and its Trump-hating targets. Trump should have expected this and not "mused" out loud. By the way, that term "musing," was used by the liberal-leaning VOX news organization covering the hoopla. Not my description, but it fits. Musers, by the way, are lazy people, thinking of what "could be," usually with a bong to their lips, while other folks work.

But the horses are out of the barn and the MSM and other Trump-haters are having a field day, almost giddy with Trump's musings. "He is telling Americans to inject Lysol" I have seen this morning in memes and posts. "If just one person dies from Trump's stupidity, the blood will be on his hands" was another gem.

Let's be clear, from what experts say, ingesting common disinfectants is, on its face a pretty bad idea. I found this nugget on the Internet: Every year between 2012 and 2016, poison control centers in the U.S. received 43,000 to 46,000 calls related to household bleach, from calls about accidental or other ingestion to inhalation of fumes, researchers reported in 2019 in the journal Clinical Toxicology. The researchers point out "those who ingest a large amount of a dilute formulation or a high concentration preparation [of bleach] can develop severe, and rarely fatal, corrosive injury."

Ah hell, what is another death from some stupid person drinking a shot of Lysol or Clorox when in totality, Trump is "responsible" for ALL the 50K-plus deaths from Covid-9 or 19, according to **The Washington Post** columnist Jennifer Rubin last week. Of course, that "dead pool" includes some 3,000 New Yorkers that "just died" but were added to the "mix" without any Coronavirus signs or symptoms. Why not? Last night a guy was shot in neighboring Phoenix, and on his deathbed, he whispered "Covid-9, Covid-9, I buried Paul." (Most will not get that one. It was a personal nugget for me and my big brother.)

So yes, I said President Trump was stupid. That is a bit harsh. Maybe, naïve is a better choice, for him thinking he could "think out loud." Well, Mr. President, thinking out loud is oxygen for those that hate you. Zip it.

So, what did President Trump ACTUALLY say? Here tis: "Supposing we hit the body with a tremendous, whether it's ultraviolet or just very powerful light ... and then I said supposing you brought the light inside the body, which you can do either through the skin or in some other way. And I think you said you're gonna test that," Trump said, addressing the Coronavirus Task Force in the press briefing. "And then I see disinfectant, where it knocks it (Coronavirus) out in a minute, one minute, and is there a way we can do something like that by injection inside, or almost a cleaning. Because you see, it gets in the lungs and it does a tremendous number on the lungs, so it'd be interesting to check that. So, that you're going to have to use medical doctors with, but it sounds interesting to me."

The most important line in that rambling musing was "you're going to have to use medical doctors...but it sounds interesting." Thus, the "musing."

What didn't he say? "Americans SHOULD inject disinfectants." "Americans SHOULD inject Lysol." NOW!

Again, he was "musing," and I hope he learned his lesson considering the rabid mentality of today's Trump-hating media and other 24/7/365 Trump haters. The Left will continue to use his "musing" as a hammer from now until Election Day with the mantra, as I said earlier, "if just one person dies from this, it is all on Trump."

Funny, in the time it took me to write this post, about 30 minutes, 53 healthy yet harmless unborn babies were murdered, according to statistics, half by Planned Parenthood. Gosh, no "outrage" there. But, of course, I digress. Purposefully.

CHANNELING RAHM: NEVER LET A DISTRACTION "WASTE" A CRISIS

Former Obama Chief-of-Staff Rahm Emmanuel once famously said, "Never let a crisis go to waste." If he were alive today, he would modify that quote. No wait! He is alive, just not relevant after his disastrous tenure as the Mayor of Chicago where he turned seemingly everyone against him, and crime soared in the Windy City.

Regardless, a Democrat operative to the core, Emmanuel in today's hyper-divided U.S. might say: "Never let a DISTRACTION waste a crisis."

The crisis the Democrats, led by House Speaker Nancy Pelosi they, don't want to waste is the Coronavirus pandemic, without question the biggest health and financial crisis of our lives. Yes Virginia, believe it or not, this crisis is bigger than Trump when he wasn't President sleeping with porn star Stormy Daniels and then paying her off. This one is real, and tens of thousands are dead in this country and millions of Americans are suffering financially like never before.

The DISTRACTION this time? I'll get to that in a minute.

But first, the DISTRACTIONS that got in the way of previous "crises" the Dems were certain would bring President Trump down. There was "Russia, Russia, Russia." As a host of, no wait, ALL the MSM talking heads told us, the "obvious" collusion between Team Trump and the Russians to sway the 2016 election, meant "the walls are closing in on Trump." They gleefully opined each day that "this was the beginning of the end."

The DISTRACTION? An economy that was just starting to rock and roll. By the end of the Mueller investigation, which found no collusion, the economy was in the Rock and Roll Hall of Fame right next to Buddy Holly and Elvis: job growth, wage growth and 401Ks through the roof. Oh, and ISIS as a caliphate was kaput.

The next crisis that would certainly "kill" The Donald was a single phone call with the Ukrainian President, with lots of folks listening in. The DISTRACTION? Joe Biden's crackhead son was found to be making large coin off the Ukrainians and Daddy Joe had threatened to financially punish the Ukrainians on video tape. Regardless of the distraction, the Dems put their heads down and kept going all the way to an impeachment, led by a totally unlikeable Congressman Adam Schiff, that failed miserably and only strengthened Trump's hand.

All was well in the Land of Trump entering 2020, a Presidential election year, and the Dems were running on fumes. Their prospective candidates to unseat Trump were a modern day Keystone Cops: an avowed Socialist who honeymooned in the Soviet Union, a wacky Senator who falsely claimed she was a Native American, a platitude-spewing Indiana mayor who reminded us daily that he was a gay Christian (Yeah, we get and it's not an issue Pete!), and the old reliable horse on the farm, Joe Biden, who couldn't construct a coherent sentence nor remember the state in which he was campaigning at the time.

And then, it hit. The China Virus. The Wuhan Virus. The Coronavirus. Covid-19, or as Joe Biden called it Covid-9. It was real and it was deadly, especially if you were elderly and/ or had pre-existing conditions. Finally, the Democrats had a legitimate crisis they could use to their advantage and they waited nary a millisecond, as Rahm told them, "letting it go to waste."

As the Chinese Communist government, aided by the buffoons (some would say crooks) at the World Health Organization (WHO), continued to lie about the deadliness and human-to-human transferability of the virus that began, without question, in some way or another in China, the Trump Administration formed a virus task force on January 28th. Three days later, Trump, ignoring the advice of his top scientist on his task force, Anthony Fauci, closed all travel from China to the United States. Italy did the same.

Within minutes, leading Dem presidential candidate Joe Biden scoffed at Trump's action against China, calling it "xenophobic."

Actually, what Biden said was typically incoherent: "This is no time for Donald Trump's record of hysteria and xenophobia, hysterical xenophobia, to uh, and fear mongering." Got that? Other Dem pols, at the national and state level, fell in line and started to pummel Trump and as the infections and deaths grew daily, the Dems had the crisis they had worked so hard to get, to get Trump.

New York Governor Andrew Cuomo became a "must-see-TV" star with his handling of the crisis in his state, ground zero for the virus infections and deaths. The media fawned over him; his composure, his intelligence and his compassion, they said, all dwarfed what the "killer" in the "chaotic" White House was doing. Of course, the crisis which Cuomo wasn't "wasting," eventually got a DISTRACTION when it was revealed that Cuomo had approved sending virus-infected elderly people back in their retirement community or long-term care facility, spreading the virus and killing more people. Perhaps thousands. Of course, Cuomo "blamed" the move on his health chief Howard Zucker. The buck stopped, ah, over there, dammit!

But that would not be the only DISTRACTION that got in the way of the Dems "not wasting" this crisis. Michigan Governor Gretchen Whitmer, an early bet to become Biden's running mate in November, got rave reviews for her get-tough approach to "protect" her citizens until she went a bridge too far. Make that about four or five bridges too far. She banned the sale of garden seeds at Home Depots, declared golf off limits, and forbid folks from visiting their relatives or the old lady next door in the Mitten State. She basically put a ban on living in the name of safety, unless of course you wanted to buy weed or a lottery ticket or were itching to get an abortion.

That's right, despite ordering a halt to elective surgeries in the state, Whitmer wanted to keep abortions going because, in her words, abortion was a "life-sustaining" procedure. I am not making this up. She said it. Proudly.

When I first started writing about Whitmer, as her edicts became wackier by the day, I called her Governor Almond Joy: sometimes you feel like a nut, sometimes you don't. (Sing it with me, everyone!) After her "life-sustaining" abortion quote, I will forever remember her as the "Killer Queen."

But the beat went on, especially among the MSM, even as the virus crisis began to slowly, painfully ebb, with MSNBC, CNN, **The New York Times** and **The Washington Post** using quotes, any quotes, from "experts" that claimed the worst was not behind us. In fact, as one "expert" noted recently, we are in for something like the "Winter from Hell." Oh, and it is ALL Trump's fault. Not the Chinese, and certainly not those caring folks at the WHO. Trump and Trump alone is to blame. The xenophobe's chickens have finally come home to roost. This would finally, finally "kill" him.

And then, the Mother of all DISTRACTIONS appeared and went over like a pregnant pole vaulter. It was revealed that there was a list of some 16 Obama Administration officials that had "unmasked" the identity of "disgraced" former Lt. General Mike Flynn, whom Trump had fired in early 2017 for lying to VP Mike Pence. Flynn, selected as Trump's National Security Advisor, had been talking (once) to the Russian Ambassador during the transition period before Trump took office. Egad! When the news first hit of this "list," the names of the 16 Obama "unmaskers" was not yet public. We only knew it had to do with unmasking Flynn.

What would the Dems do with this horrible DISTRACTION? Everything about "not wasting a crisis" had been going so well. Trump just wasn't on the ropes; he had been knocked out of the ring into the third row of seats. Ah, an answer: Good 'ol Joe Biden, tucked away in his basement at his home in Delaware, watching old reruns of "Conjunction Junction" to better hone his speaking skills.

Biden appeared on what should have been a safe haven for him: ABC's "Good Morning America" with host and former Clinton Administration bigwig George Stephanopoulos. If you see George in the shower, there is a big "D" on his hairy little Greek chest, although it is not recommended. George asked Biden if he knew anything about the INVESTIGATION into General Flynn and Biden pled ignorance and began railing that this story was just a DISTRACTION when Trump should be focused on the virus crisis.

And then the wheels came off the wagon. For some strange reason, Stephanopoulos suddenly found his unbiased-journalist gonads and went back at Biden and reminded the former VP that he was supposedly in a White House meeting where the Flynn investigation was discussed. Busted, Biden feigned that the audio plug in his ear was malfunctioning, hemmed and hawed (and I believe slightly soiled himself) and finally fessed up that he knew a bit about the Flynn investigation. But that was it! Trust him!

They say timing is everything, and for Biden, it was everything bad. The next day, the list of 16 Obama unmaskers was publicly revealed and Biden's name popped out like a seventh-grade boy's zit. The DISTRACTION had just gotten worse.

So, what to do, what to do, the Dems thought, fearing their perfect virus crisis was evaporating like Stormy, Russia and the Ukraine. Wait, they thought, we still have the media. Quickly, Dem operatives fanned out across the land to beg the MSM to help them "keep hope (the crisis) alive."

But begging was not needed. The MSM was already fully engaged.

Over the past three-plus years, Team Trump had called both the Russian collusion charge and the Ukrainian quid pro quo allegation, hoaxes, and the MSM ridiculed them for it, again, citing the end was near both times for Trump. But, this "unmasking" scandal, they screamed on EVERY channel, is a TRUE hoax and a crazy conspiracy theory that Trump won't get away with. They laughed at Trump for calling the DISTRACTION "Obamagate." They even trotted out the proven liar and Trump hater James Clapper to convince us all that Trump's claims were frivolous.

Perhaps CNN's Wolf Blitzer said it best, accusing Trump of having a preoccupation with former President Obama and his potential role in this "made up" unmasking scandal.

Well, Wolf, Trump does, and my guess is so will tens of millions of other Americans as we learn more about this "DISTRACTION," despite the MSM's best effort to make it go away so that the Dems don't have to "waste" yet another crisis.

OBAMA GETS TACKY, TYPICALLY DIVISIVE AS CNN FAILS JOURNALISM 101

Usually commencement speeches are uplifting and challenging, and not "Debbie-Downers." Oops, that was probably misogynistic. My bad. I meant "Darrell-Downers." But there was former President Barack Obama, addressing "all sorts of folks" during the online commencement for thousands of Historically Black Colleges and Universities (HBCU) graduates.

Uplifting? If you consider a former President "bitch-slapping" a current President in a time of national and international crisis the likes we haven't seen 80 years UPLIFTING, well, I guess those graduates got their money's worth. (Oops, there I go again with the misogyny. Damn!)

"More than anything, this (Coronavirus) pandemic has fully, finally torn back the curtain that so many of the folks in charge know what they're doing. A lot of them aren't even pretending to be in charge," former President Barack Obama told thousands of HBCU young people "non-gathered" around their computer screen.

It was not the first time Mr. Obama had taken a swipe at the Trump Administration in the last few days. Earlier, Mr. Obama had publicly called the crisis response from the Trump team "an absolute chaotic disaster."

If you are a modern-Presidential historian, Obama's multiple attacks of President Trump within a week in a time of national crisis were unprecedented. If you are me, they were beyond tacky, harmful to our country and punk-like in that setting. Considering his audience yesterday, predominantly Black, and the fact that the Black community in this country has been impacted disproportionally by the Coronavirus deaths, it was also extremely divisive. But then, that was fuel for President Obama in all his eight years in office.

But Jason, please, as Rodney Dangerfield said while bribing the referee in his golf match with Judge Smails in Caddyshack, "Keep it fair! Keep it fair!"

OK, to be fair, President Trump has blistered Mr. Obama, most recently describing the whole General Flynn/ Russia, Russia, Russia debacle as "Obamagate," and has criticized the Obama Administration for depleting the National Stock Pile (of health crisis supplies) and not replenishing it. Trump's charges against Obama are ALLEGATIONS. Remember that word.

So, yesterday on CNN's "The Situation Room with Wolf Blitzer," ol' Wolf reported Obama's slam during his commencement speech and then went live to CNN White House correspondent Jeremy Diamond. Diamond reported the White House response to Obama's criticism and then decided it was his "duty" to defend the former President.

"The TRUTH is…there were certain items (in the National Stock Pile) that were not replenished," he said. "But by no means was it completely depleted."

OK, maybe the President was exaggerating a bit, but here is the TRUTH, CNN. According to FactCheck.org, no friend of the Trump Administration, "It's true that some of the supplies in the stockpile that governors are currently asking the government to send to states were not completely restocked during Obama's presidency.

"For example, *The Washington Post* reported on March 10 that the reserves of the N95 respirator masks were not 'significantly restored' after tens of millions of the devices were distributed from the stockpile during the H1N1 influenza pandemic of 2009.

"Greg Burel, who was the director of the Strategic National Stockpile for more than 12 years until he retired in January, recently told CBS News: "We didn't receive funds to replace those masks, protective gear and the anti-virals that we used for H1N1.

"He told Vice News that he decided to use the program's limited funding to instead purchase vaccines, flu medications and other pharmaceuticals…

"…the Obama administration's attempts to add more equipment, such as ventilators, to the stockpile were not successful."

So, the two key health safety items in combating the Coronavirus, masks and ventilators, were depleted and replenishment by the Obama Administration, for some reason, was unsuccessful. Period. So much for the TRUTH, CNN.

Back to yesterday's "The Situation Room" episode and yes, I did a no-no and buried one of the leads. At the end of the segment, when Blitzer, I believe, mentioned the term, "Obamagate," correspondent Jeremy Diamond responded that Trump was throwing out "BASELESS CHARGES." (Note: I say "believe" because I saw the segment live once and that particular segment of the piece was mysteriously edited out of the clip currently on CNN's "The Situation Room" website. Hmmm.)

"BASELESS CHARGES"? An unbiased journalist would call Trump's claims against Obama, ALLEGATIONS. But here, Diamond and CNN ARE, as so typical in today's MSM, acting as judge, jury and executioner. Just think back to earlier this year during the failed impeachment of Trump. The MSM led by CNN, in toto, called ALLEGATIONS against Joe Biden and his son Hunter concerning shaky dealings in the Ukraine as "completely DEBUNKED," despite the fact they hadn't been, whatsoever. Again, judge, jury and executioner.

"Obamagate" and the Bidens' bad behavior in the Ukraine are ALLEGATIONS, period. They are not BASELESS CHARGES, nor are either of them DEBUNKED, despite the biased "opinion" of a supposed "news" organization. This is why CNN continues to fail Journalism 101.

But then, in reality, they don't care.

CUOMO ACCEPTS BLAME FOR ELDERLY DEATHS…AH, NOT!

New York Governor Andrew Cuomo didn't get his "15 minutes of fame" that everyone will get sooner or later according to the late Andy Warhol. He got 15 weeks. Now that "fame" is starting to get chipped away.

Initially, it appeared that Cuomo's newfound fame had no end in sight. Check that. It HAD an end in sight: replacing Joe Biden as the nominee on the Democratic Presidential ticket. The media, especially CNN and MSNBC, went "Lady Gaga" over Cuomo and dutifully broadcast every single minute of every single morning press conference he held, declaring him the leader that America needed in this crisis, certainly compared to the Orangeman in a "chaotic" White House that "didn't know what it was doing."

Yep, Cuomo was saving New York and, hell, America while President Trump was, according to The Washington Post columnist Jennifer Rubin personally "responsible" for the tens of thousands of deaths at the hands of the Coronavirus.

"Cuomo Love" became so intense that he was being called "America's Governor." And Cuomo soaked it in. As the days passed, his daily press briefings went from information and guidance solely to some information and "inspiring" family stories about his mama's world-famous meatballs and the fact that he really "liked" his daughter's new boyfriend. And, he brought the family dog into the mix, noting that his little four-legged friend was showing signs of depression. I'm not sure if Fido was ever suicidal, but there were reports of The Suicide Hotline in Albany getting a mysterious call where the caller simply said, "Woof, woof, woof." (I made up that last part, as I am not certain what the dog actually said.)

Cuomo was single-handedly saving New York despite one stupid decision after another by the mayor of the largest city in the state and ground zero for the pandemic, New York City. Mayor deBalsio became even more of a joke than he already was pre-pandemic and outdid his nutty self when he told NYers to videotape or photograph fellow NYers NOT adhering to social distancing directives and send the evidence to him so that his Big Apple Gestapo could "take care" of these obvious domestic terrorists. "Ve have vays of making you social distance!"

Mayor Big Bird's "Big Brother" tactics came at the time when New York was trying to empty its jails and prisons of convicted criminals who had been infected with the Coronavirus. NYers, a tough bunch, responded to DeBlasio, sending him a slew of evidence, not of social distancing criminals, but rather hundreds of images of "penises" and "Adolph Hitler." Ach Tung, Mayor Big Bird, ya cheese weenie!

Now, early on Cuomo wasn't perfect. He mockingly complained that the White House (read: Trump) wasn't getting enough of the desperately needed ventilators to his state, only to get a bit of egg on his face when it was discovered that 4.000 new, unused ventilators were idly sitting in a NYC warehouse across the Hudson River in New Jersey. Oops. For the foreseeable next few weeks, Cuomo played nice with the White House. He knew where his Italian breadstick was buttered.

Throughout March and most of April, Cuomo's star continued to shine bright. That notion of him replacing Biden on the Democratic ticket was not a pipe dream, but a distinct possibility with every new gaffe that came out of the former Vice President's mouth and, of course the "Finger Puppet" allegations of sexual abuse. But that star took a major, perhaps lethal blow on April 20th when a **New York Post** reporter had the "audacity" to ask him about the March 25 edict forcing the admittance of Coronavirus-infected elderly folk BACK into their retirement homes or long-term care facilities. The ensuing deaths of the elderly in those facilities is estimated to represent 25 percent of the death toll in New York thus far.

Cuomo's answer to the reporter's question about the deadly policy: "That's a good question. I don't know." Stunning to say the least from the man that had, according to the MSM Cuomo worshippers, ALL the answers, all the compassion and all the leadership that President Trump was sorely missing.

But Cuomo DID have an answer; it just took him a day to formulate it. The next day he threw Howard Zucker, his state health commissioner, under a NY Transit bus and claimed it was Zucker who had instituted the policy, one that Cuomo "didn't know," about. Sacrificial lamb Howard Zucker had even promised "if you are positive, you should be admitted back to a nursing home. The necessary precautions will be taken to protect the other residents there."

Yeah, right.

So where are we, where is Cuomo today? Yesterday, the Governor pulled his health commissioner from under bus, brushed him off, and decided it was "no more Mr. Nice Guy" with the President of the United States. This disaster among the elderly was not his fault, nor Zucker's, but was New York just following the protocols ordered by "The White House and the CDC."

Yeah, that's the ticket.

It is apparent that the man who put on his "big boy pants" to become a modern-day Messiah, had scrapped that outfit, preferring to don one of those cute Bavarian-style shorts with built-in suspenders my wife put on my boys when they were toddlers.

Governor Cuomo, you need to call *The Washington Post's* Jennifer Rubin and ask for a correction of her April 15th column where she puts all the Coronavirus deaths on Trump's bloody hands and attribute a few thousand of those deaths to you, or, er, Health Commissioner Zucker, or, um, the "White House and the CDC."

Oh, never mind. After all, even if you "were" the new Messiah, Mr. Cuomo, you can't raise the dead.

NEW YORK TIMES AND DEMS HAVE PARANOID PANTIES IN A BUNCH

Unreported thus far, but in reading a long "news" article in yesterday's *The New York Times*, I have come to the conclusion that a side effect of the Coronavirus, whether or not you are actually infected, is EXTREME ELECTION PARANOIA.

The major piece in the "news" paper focused on the FACT that some Democratic strategists, including professors from extremely expensive institutions of "higher" learning, are seriously playing out "doomsday" scenarios: where President Trump uses the pandemic to rob Americans of a "free and fair" election this November and remains in office indefinitely in the worst case, or make it extremely difficult if not impossible for Joe Biden to enter the White House in the best case scenario.

Here's one doomsday scenario *The New York Times* offered up in the very first paragraph of their "news" story:

"In October, President Trump declares a state of emergency in major cities in battleground states, like Milwaukee and Detroit, banning polling places from opening.

"A week before the election, Attorney General William P. Barr announces a criminal investigation into the Democratic presidential nominee, Joseph R. Biden Jr.

"After Mr. Biden wins a narrow Electoral College victory, Mr. Trump refuses to accept the results, won't leave the White House and declines to allow the Biden transition team customary access to agencies before the Jan. 20 inauguration."

I won't call this story "fake news," which it most certainly is, but in reading the story it reminded me of the movie "War Games," in which a super computer named Joshua plays out various war scenarios to determine which, if any, countries will survive in the advent of a global thermonuclear war. This is what these geniuses in the Democratic Party, along with their university allies are doing with, I assume, Trump representing the Russians and good 'ol Joe Biden representing the U.S.A. in a thermonuclear electoral war.

Far-fetched conspiracy theories? Not according to ***The New York Times***. The Dems are "outraged by Mr. Trump, and fearful that he might try to disrupt the campaign before, during and after Election Day." They are playing these "war games," The Times opines, "as Mr. Trump and his administration abandon longstanding political norms."

Oh, I get it. These folks aren't paranoid because, again according to ***The Times***, Trump and his gang are bad, bad, bad. Remember, this is "news" according to the "news" paper.

The paranoia has gotten white-hot recently "as the president continues to attack the integrity of mail voting, and insinuates that the election system is rigged." They also find it disturbing that Trump is regurgitating "UNFOUNDED claims of voter fraud." Unfounded? Really? I would suggest these claims are not "unfounded," but rather ignored by the Gray Lady and other Trump haters.

"In the eight to 10 months I've been yapping at people about this stuff, the reactions have gone from, 'Don't be silly, that won't happen,' to an increasing sense of, 'You know, that could happen,'" Rosa Brooks, a Georgetown University law professor told The Times. I agree with Rosa: she is yapping, something all quality professors do when they are promoting their political agenda. God help us if her thoughts are making their way into her classroom. Oh snap, too late!

The "news" paper found Marc Elias, a Washington lawyer who leads the Democratic National Committee's legal efforts to fight "voter suppression" measures. He told The Times, that "not a day goes by when he doesn't field a question from senior Democratic officials about whether Mr. Trump could postpone or cancel the election."

Elias spells out the paranoia rattling around in his noggin. Trump might change the date of the election, or worse yet, he could make it extremely difficult for "people" to vote in urban centers (read: that old chestnut, Republican racism against minorities) in key states. Hell, Elias surmises that Trump might go so far as to use the Coronavirus pandemic to declare a state of emergency and use the National Guard and throw down the gauntlet on gatherings of more than ten people. Wow, on the latter, Elias has confused Trump with the heavy-handed edicts of several Democratic governors regarding church services.

The paranoia has made its way into the Biden Presidential campaign team, and Biden himself.

"Since 2016, Donald Trump has shown that he is always ready to sacrifice our basic democratic norms for his personal and political interests," said Bob Bauer, a Biden senior adviser.

There goes that "basic democratic norms" line again. Boy, they like that line.

"We ASSUME he may well resort to any kind of trick, ploy or scheme he can in order to hold onto his presidency," Bauer continued. "We have built a strong program to plan for and address every possibility to ensure that he does not succeed."

Well, Bob, you know what happens when you ASSUME.

The Democratic paranoia has not gone unnoticed by Team Trump. "Hillary Clinton, Stacey Abrams and the entire Democratic Party refused to accept the results of their elections and pushed the Russia collusion conspiracy theory for years," said Tim Murtaugh, the communications director for Mr. Trump's re-election campaign. "Now, Joe Biden's allies have formed actual conspiracy committees where they'll work up new hoaxes to further undermine our democracy. They are wasting their time. As President Trump has repeatedly said, the election will happen on Nov. 3."

The Dems' paranoia and their doomsday war games might end up taking their eyes off the ball. I suggest their time would be better spent working with their torch bearer, Joe Biden. Give him a map of the U.S. and circle the place he is going to each time he travels. Have 'ol Joe to watch reruns of ABC TV's grade school show "Conjunction Junction" to become at least somewhat coherent when he speaks. And remind him that "voting" for Trump does not remove the "blackness" from African Americans.

BIDEN IS RUBBER, TRUMP IS GLUE

Days after Democratic Presidential candidate Joe Biden stepped in "it" big time, telling a black radio host that if black people don't vote "for him," well, they "ain't black," 'ol Joe has wiped off his shoe and has smeared "it" on his November opponent, President Trump. Biden, in an op-ed for Bloomberg, accused Trump of "racializing" the Coronavirus pandemic and promoting hatred against Asian Americans by calling the virus "the Chinese virus."

The op-ed, co-authored by Biden's potential running mate for the White House, Illinois Senator Tammy Duckworth, spoke of the horrors of harassment Asian Americans have faced throughout the pandemic. They wrote "Asian Americans have been blamed for COVID-19: yelled at by strangers in parking lots, refused service at stores and needlessly, cruelly scapegoated by the most powerful man on the planet, President Donald Trump, who has racialized the pandemic and stoked xenophobia every time he's uttered the term 'Chinese virus'."

For the life of me, in my numerous trips to grocery stores, WalMarts, Home Depots and Sam's Clubs in my new home of Metro Phoenix, an area with a large Asian American population, I have not seen or heard of a single xenophobic incident toward Asian Americans.

Oh, I know, I just probably have my "white privilege" blinders on. They came as a gift when I ordered by Confederate flag face mask online from Racists R Us. Ahem.

Nowhere in the op-ed did Biden and Duckworth consider the reason Trump called it the "Chinese virus." Chinese sources early on in the pandemic, spread a conspiracy theory that COVID-19 was the brainchild of the U.S. military, secretly planted in the Wuhan lab, prompting the President to call it what everyone knew: it was a virus that began in and was spread by China while the Communist government, aided and abetted by the World Health Organization, played hide-the-wonton.

I am certain that Joe's co-authored op-ed drew cheers in the halls of the Chinese Communist Party headquarters. After all, those "fair-minded" folks called Trump a racist when he first called the Coronavirus the "Chinese Virus." Trump, the communist leaders claimed, was wrongly attacking "Chinese people" and "Asian Americans" for the horrible pandemic.

Of course, he was not. In March, Trump tweeted: "It is very important that we totally protect our Asian American community in the United States, and all around the world. They are amazing people, and the spreading of the Virus is NOT their fault in any way, shape, or form. They are working closely with us to get rid of it. WE WILL PREVAIL TOGETHER!" And later, in a press conference, Trump warned that he would not allow harassment of Asian Americans saying, "I'm not going to let that happen."

In their op-ed, Biden and Duckworth recalled the "sad history of racism against Asian Americans," but 'ol Joe, a quarter-century older than Duckworth, should have recalled the actual history of prejudice against Asian Americans the time it happened "bigly" and "Official U.S. Policy" when DEMOCRAT President Franklin D. Roosevelt threw Asian Americans into concentration camps during World War II. Oh, my bad, they were called "internment camps," and Joe was just a youngster at the time.

Biden was not finished making a fool of himself in the op-ed. He and Duckworth talked about Asian Americans being a part of "one community." You get it: Chinese Americans, Vietnamese Americans and Japanese Americans are all the same. (Yes, I realize Trump called "them" a "community," but he IS a racist, dammit!) I wouldn't be surprised to learn that in an early draft of the op-ed, 'ol Joe wrote, "hell, they all look alike."

Far-fetched thought? No way, not after his "you ain't black" racist gaffe.

CHAPTER THREE

DEMOCRATS GONE WILD!

THE GOOD, BAD AND THE UGLY DURING THE VIRUS CRISIS…SO FAR

Wow, what a week during the CHINESE Corona Virus.

The Good

Neighbors helping neighbors, and even strangers.

People acting civilly while shopping and not going bat s--t when the toilet paper is gone from the grocery store in a New York minute.

Speaking of toilet paper, by making people stay at home, they are wiping with Northern, Charmin and Cottonelle, instead of the commercial stuff in restaurants and offices that contains wood chips and glass shards and most likely asbestos. Your bunghole thanks you. Mr. Whipple is smiling down from Heaven.

No riots or panic (except in Iran, but then, they have a lot to protest beyond the virus).

North Korea has "ZERO" cases of Corona Virus. Way to go Kim!! I guess the Dick-Tator has a brilliant plan of killing its citizens before they can contract the virus. Brilliant I say! Just brilliant!

A slew of unrelated companies, from GM to GE and many others, have turned their businesses over to make ventilators and masks. Think about it, would you ever think that you'd be happy wearing a mask made by underwear giant Hanes. Question: are those boxer or briefs masks and do they come with a kangaroo pouch?

The Bad

Many in the MSM cannot get over their Trump Derangement Syndrome. NY Guv Cuomo has and in the meantime is doing a pretty damn fine job for his state and, yes, the country. He had a minor misstep when he chastised the White House for not getting enough ventilators to his state, only to find out 4,000 ventilators for NYC were resting peacefully, unused, in a warehouse across the Hudson. Since then, not a single slap at the White House that I have heard. By the way, his daily press conferences are useful, but I wish he would pontificate a bit less (actually a lot less) and I don't need to hear about his mother's meat balls.

Put Trump-hater CA Guv Newson in the same boat as Cuomo – taking care of the citizens of their state and putting politics aside. As Lili von Shtupp in Blazing Saddles said: "It is wefweshing."

Not much so for the likes of CNN's Don Lemon and MSNBC's Rachel Maddow. Maddow is constantly on the TDS I.V. drip and has embarrassed herself. When Trump announced one of the Navy hospital ships would be in NY in a week, she laughed and laughed and laughed, claiming it would take weeks and weeks. The ship arrived in NY in 10 days.

Adding insult to injury, Maddow has been calling for Trump to stop his daily Virus Team press briefings. Of course, they continue despite the fact her network has decided not to broadcast them. Oh, that would be something useful to her viewers, but then who cares about those 15 people. Funny, had Trump decided NOT to do daily press conferences on the biggest health crisis of our times, Maddow would have been first in line, blaming the President for a lack of leadership.

Regarding CNN's Lemon, well, a day doesn't go by that he doesn't, multiple times, call Trump a liar during his low-ratings broadcast. Remember, this is the "news" anchor that laughed, wiping fake tears from his eyes and putting his head on the desk, because his guests were referring to Trump supporters by the usual charges of mouth-breathing, ignorant, racists, etc.

Wrapping up the bad, likely Democratic Presidential nominee,

Uncle Joe Biden, in an interview, referred to the Chinese city/ region where the virus likely began, Wuhan, as "Luhan".

Oh, that's right, he has an excuse: he stuttered as a kid. For the life of me I cannot recall any stutterer I have ever known that replaced "Ws" with "Ls". I guess, you ain't seen nothin' yet, ba-ba-ba-baby, baby, you ain't seen noth-noth-nothin yet.

The Ugly

CA Congressthing Maxine Waters, who called for Trump's impeachment BEFORE he was inaugurated, this week said Trump's handling of the virus crisis proved "You're (Trump) not knowledgeable & you don't know more than experts & generals. Your ignorance & incompetence are appalling & you continue to demonstrate that every time you open your mouth!" I guess Maxine said this while looking in a mirror. I wish I could take her out for a drink and explain the situation. Hey Maxine, join me, the Water and Vinegar cocktail you obviously need is on me.

Hillary Clinton, while almost single-handedly keeping the boxed wine industry afloat, went beyond ugly and seriously hurt her chances to be voted in as the 2020 Democratic nominee at the likely brokered Democratic Convention in Swillwaukee this summer. Currently those odds stand at 1 in 1 Gazillion. Hillary had most likely drained a tainted Boto Box Chardonnay and decided to tweet once the U.S. death toll from the virus topped the rest of the other countries infected. She tweeted that Trump had kept his promise to "make America First."

According to my truly unreliable sources, Hillary attempted to get Bubba Clinton's advice before launching the nasty tweet. She allegedly knocked on the locked bedroom door and Bubba responded, "Hey, honey britches, I am kind busy (Are the ropes too tight on your wrists, girls?). Go with whatever you think is right. You are the best,

Hill."

Fox's Greg Gutfeld said Hillary should "rot in Hell" for her post. However, moments later, there was a riot in Hell, led by Adolf Hitler and Jeffrey Epstein, and Satan announced a Hillary Immigration Ban, effective immediately or until Hell freezes over.

AGAIN, WHY I LOVE THIS COUNTRY

I was in Target, early this morning. The line for toilet paper was long, yet civil. Maybe because the victors scored "mega" rolls of Cottonelle, Northern and those bastards at Charmin; not the four-pack !!!! I paid nine thousand dollars for at Walmart the other day. I, smartly, had my poopy moment in the Target restroom while keeping up on the Internet. The TP there was, well, cruel, but free.

I was not in Target to get TP, although I was tempted to get in the line just for the helluva it. But I passed. I was in Target for balls, golf balls. Yes, in the era of this pandemic, I am playing golf with my wife and daughter this afternoon.

Talk about social distancing! I slice like a MoFo and my wife and daughter hit it right down the middle of the fairway. I will be at least 100 yards from them on the second shot. Oh, shit, the third shot too. F—k, the fourth shot!!!!!!

Yes, we will be close during the putting regimen, therefore I am giving myself a "ge-mee" when I am on the green or reasonably close (100 feet). Hell, I am thinking I may par this bad motherbrother.

Bottom line from my shopping this morning: No one acting stupid at the grocery store where I bought a paper. Strangely, limiting entrance to Home Depot, although it is not a rush. Big line-up in Target for TP, although everyone was pleasant.

Funny, I saw an article yesterday that said TP was NOT an "essential" item. Really? Change the first "E" to "A" in essential and you get my drift, ha, or my roll.

I LOVE TO COUNT!!!!!

I'm seriously trying to figure out why the Left, ah, the Trump Haters, have determined that Trump and his Administration have FAILED during the Chinese (Ghina!!!) Virus Crisis.

Let's see. As the Count on Sesame Street would do, let's COUNT THE WAYS!

ONE: Trump closed all travel from China to the U.S., first. Well kind of; Trump closed travel on January 31st, the same day as Italy, but was second to North Korea, two days earlier. Oh, I bet there are a lot of flights into North Korea on a daily basis. Oh, course, as you know by now, North Korea has "ZERO" Covid-19 cases. Zero. Oh, Kim is such a humanitarian.

TWO: The number of Trump-hating Democratic governors who are putting politics on the shelf and taking care of their citizens – NY's Andrew Cuomo and CA's Gavin Newsom.

THREE: The I.Q. of CA Congressthing Maxine Waters, who cannot grasp the idea of coming together as a nation in times of trouble.

OH! I LOVE TO COUNT!

FOUR: The actual number of people in several NY hospital waiting rooms despite the supposed panic.

FIVE: The total number of toilet paper big packs I saw a woman buying this morning at Target, going to her car, and then returning multiple times to buy more despite the imposed limit. Well, to give her a break, she had a big fat effing ass.

SIX: The number of people who touched my Mickey D's carryout "only" before handing it to me. So much for safety.

SEVEN: The number of times, each minute on his broadcast, CNN's Don Lemon calls the President of the United States a liar.

I AM STILL COUNTING!!!!

EIGHT: Eastern time, when Tucker Carlson points out all the BS on the Left.

NINE: (German) The number of good ideas the Democrats have provided during this crisis, beyond constant complaining, hang-wringing and politicizing the situation.

TEN: The job this Administration is doing for this country. Bringing unrelated businesses, big, small and medium, together in warp speed to produce needed essentials like ventilators, gowns and masks. Importantly, supporting small businesses with emergency loans (Oh, media crowed THIS morning that small biz loans were not available a DAY, yes, just one frickin' day, after program went online. Geez. Initial Obamacare website was broken for weeks, if not months, if not forever. A day? Give me an effing break.

Two massive Navy hospital ships with thousands of beds and tons of medical supplies, in days, not weeks, in LA and NY. Temporary hospitals built in record speed at Javits Center and in Central Park (thanks to Samaritan's Purse – Oh, those damned Christians!!!). Etc., etc., etc.

JUST AS WE SUSPECTED, THE CORONA VIRUS IS RACIST

It took them awhile, but MSNBC has come to the conclusion that the Corona virus is, yes, racist. Reports show that 70 percent of the deaths in Louisiana and 40 percent of the deaths in Michigan are among African Americans. Of course, the deaths in those two states are centered in two minority-majority cities – New Orleans and Detroit.

Likewise, the majority of deaths in New York are in minority-majority boroughs of the metropolis, namely Queens and The Bronx.

Congressperson Ayanna Pressley, Democrat from Massachusetts and a member of AOC's "Squad," has headlined a letter to HHS Secretary Azar asking for "equal treatment" for African Americans despite ZERO evidence this group of Americans is being "treated" any differently than white folks.

Now, while it is true that African Americans, especially African American men, have a disproportionate share of one underlying illness, diabetes, making them more susceptible to acquiring the virus, I guess we must conclude that those "honest" Chinese who hatched and hid this virus before spreading it around the globe are, at their core, racists.

Meanwhile, one media outlet has reported that some outspoken African American leaders are calling for African Americans, especially men, NOT to wear masks for fear they will be wrongly mistaken for criminals. No, I am not making this up. I guess "if the mask ain't on, you've done nothin' wrong."

Finally, there is absolutely no evidence that the current surge upward in the stock market impacts only the stocks held by white folks.

Finally, finally, this just in: CNN's Anderson Cooper has definitively determined that the Corona virus deaths are all Trump's fault. It is the closure we all need. Thank you, Anderson.

THE FIRST DEMOCRATIC NATIONAL COMMITTEE MEETING NOW THAT BERNIE IS TOAST
SATIRE

When this terrible Coronavirus crisis is over – and most, but not all sadly, hope soon – I wish I could be a fly on the wall at the first meeting of the Democratic National Committee since the crisis began. The Chair of the DNC is Tony Perez. He is the former Secretary of Labor under Obama, which has nothing to do with labor during birth – the Left hates that and gives tons of money to avoid this grief, actually an inconvenience. Ahem.

Perez also likes to swear a lot in public settings, so I can only assume in closed-door meetings he is fluent in profanity. (Yes, I have a PhD in profanity, by the way.) For the ease of typing purposes, I will refer to Chairman Perez, appropriately, as TP, in my vision of the upcoming first meeting.

TP: Come to order, come to order. Dammit, Alexandria Whatever Cortez, sit the f—k down and shut up…for once! Same to you too Tashida Rlaib.

MICHIGAN CONGRESSTHING TLAIB: It's Rashida Tlaib! Perhaps we need to impeach you, M-therfu—er!

TP: OK, OK, settle, settle. I know that nerves, right now, are raw, but we have to circle the tents and figure out where we go from here.

SENATOR LIZ WARREN: Circle the tents? Is that a reference to my fellow Native Americans?

SENATOR JOE MANCHIN: It's "circle the wagons," Pocahontas! You dumbass!

SENATOR BERNIE SANDERS: Liz, you ignoramus, I speak for many Americans, including thousands of college women who have never shaved their armpits or legs, as well, as thousands of dope-smoking 28-year-old American men who have Ancient Art degrees from seven years of college -- please, please, give up that ruse. You are not helping.

JOE BIDEN: People, people, as your new leader, let's be civil. As I sit here in Tulsa, Oklahoma --
TP: Ah, Mr. Vice President, we are in Chicago.

JOE BIDEN: Ha, ha, ha, I knew that – Chitown, Tultown, sound so similar. Anyway, as we gather here in my favorite city of Scranton, my hometown where I carried a lunch bucket, we need to figure out how we can beat Ronald Reagan in October.

TP: Jesus, help us. I give the floor to former candidate Kamala Harris, former AG of California.

SENATOR KAMALA HARRIS: Joe, honey, I love you. I know, I know, I slapped you down in the first Democratic debate, completely making up a bussing story despite the fact my parents were well-heeled, but hear me now. I desperately want to run with you. Listen, I slept my way to the top of California government with guys even older than you but trust me: I am more than willing to sleep myself back to the bottom on top of you, I mean, ahem, by your side.

JOE BIDEN: Well, I'll have to check that out with my spiritual advisor, my son, Hunter, who is in charge of screwing people without any history of knowing what he is doing. He was supposed to be in the Ukraine this week to cash a check, but he screwed up his flight and ended up in Arkansas. He will get back to you soon, but I think he sold his cell phone at a pawn shop in Little Rock. He said it was for "crackers" or some other food. Man's gotta eat! I think Napoleon said that back in 1925 during World War I.

TP: I give the "GD" floor, which seemingly is crumbling below our feet, to former South Bend mayor Pete Butta, Bitti, Betti, oh whatever the f—k your name is!

MAYOR PETE: Mr. Chairman, first, as a devout Christian, I abhor your profanity.

TP: F—k off, pal.

MAYOR PETE: Now that we have that settled, I just want to say we need to bring this country together and I would like to offer 10 platitudes that I shared during the campaign and almost single-handedly cured insomnia in our country.

SENATOR BERNIE SANDERS: Sit down, little boy!!! I poop

bigger than you! And, shave better. You look like a teenage Fred Flintstone.

TP: Bernie, Bernie, please. Now, it is my distinct honor to introduce the Speaker of the House, Nancy Pelosi.

SPEAKER PELOSI: Thank you, Mr. Chairman. Our task is simple: we must defeat this evil President. I have tried my best with an incredibly weak collusion case concerning Russia and an even weaker case concerning the Ukrainian phone call. I, being a prayerful and loving Catholic, want to apologize for not giving it my best during those two inquiries. Like all good Democrats, I have an excuse: My official sponsor, which gives me millions of dollars a year in hidden campaign contributions, Poligrip, provided me with a failed product over the past three years. My mind was NOT on Russia and later, impeachment, but on my teeth falling out. I will do better, as my new sponsor is Liquid Nails, and this sh-t can hold a boulder to a wall. Plus, I made the egregious error of putting Pencil Neck Adam Shitt, um, er, I mean, Schiff, in charge. He made Niedermeyer in Animal House look good.

JOE BIDEN: Excuse me, excuse me. I am the presumptive Democratic nominee to take on Trump this summer, ah, er, this winter or fall. I need to be heard, doggone it.

AUDIENCE: Sigh!

TP: Well, Mr. Former Vice President, we are completely behind you. It is our hope that you will join your son, Hunter, in Arkansas, and take care of your new grandbaby. Occasionally, with Secret Service protecting you, you can join your son and grandbaby watching your new daughter-in-law "on the job." It should be refreshing and will give you a new meaning of the word "poling." This meeting is adjourned.

HILLARY CLINTON: Hey, hey, what the f—k about me!! I can win! (Burp!)

DUMBEST FAMOUS HUMAN ON EARTH IDENTIFIED
SATIRE

It is official, World Health Organization (WHO) Director-General Tedros Adhanom Ghebreyesus has officially been named "Dumbest Famous Human on Earth." It was a close call, but Ghebreyesus edged out California Congresswoman Maxine Waters in a razor-thin vote and secured the "prestigious" award. The winner receives a lifetime supply of weed killer Round-Up.

The committee announcing the winner cited Ghebreyesus' recent threats to U.S. President after the President temporarily suspended U.S. funds to support the WHO. According to the most recent data, the U.S. provides a reported 22 percent of WHO's funding, by far the largest percentage of any country in the world. Per U.S. citizen, the U.S. donates 43 dollars to the WHO.

Japan, the third biggest contributor, also provides 43 dollars per citizen. Meanwhile, China, where the Coronavirus began and was hidden for weeks, is far down the list of WHO financial supporters, contributing just $1.14 per citizen to the WHO.

Ghebreyesus reacted to the suspension of U.S. support, claiming Trump's actions would result in the need for "more body bags." Considering the level of support the WHO depends on from the U.S., one award committee member said, "It was like you were flipping the bird at an ISIS killer who was holding a machete standing two feet in front of you. Super dumb."

Ghebreyesus and the WHO have come under fire recently for initially ignoring the severity of the Coronavirus until late January, despite knowing about the extent and human transfer ability as early as early December 2019. To add insult to injury, the WHO repeatedly stood by Chinese government claims that the virus was contained and therefore was "no big dear (translated, 'deal')." Arkansas Senator Tom Cotton has called for Ghebreyesus to resign and for world leaders to investigate both him and the WHO as a whole.

Meanwhile, Maxine Waters said, in a statement, she is heartbroken finishing as the runner-up. "Hell, I ain't won nothing, and this was my chance to breakthrough. Impeach 45! Impeach 45!"

Rounding out the Top Five Finalists for "Dumbest Famous Human on Earth" were:

3. NY Congresswoman Alexandria Ocasio Cortez, cited for killing 25,000 promised Amazon jobs in her home district and her frantic, screaming demand that the U.S. government provide relief checks to illegal aliens in the U.S.

4. (TIE) MSNBC's Mika Brzezinski and Joe Scarborough, citing "them being them, every day."

5. Jailed attorney Michael Avenatti, cited for, well, "Duh!"

All finalists are being awarded the same diploma given to the Scarecrow in The Wizard of Oz.

WOW! A NEW LOW -- IMPEACHING TRUMP FOR TAKING ON CORRUPTION!

A lotta hysterical and nutty Democrat "leaders" are setting their hair on fire these days. No, I am not talking about Michigan Loon Guv Gretchen Whitmer: she has great, great hair, and Joe Biden is dying to smell it and penetrate, oh hell, I won't go there. Damn My Eyes for even thinking about it! As Gomer Pyle would say, "Shame, shame, shame, Jason!" I stand corrected and look upward to the soul of Jim Nabors. (What a great human being you were while on this Earth.)

Let's set the stage, shall we? The Coronavirus was borne (next Bourne movie, I am auditioning for the lead. Heck, my name is Jason, so I think I have an "in." Plus, I am one sexy bitch who can walk up to two miles a day, now. Kind of. The construction workers in our neighborhood pick me up for the last mile. I give them losing lotto tickets. Gosh, it is such a scam on my part. Oh s--t, the guy in the pickup bed has a Glock. Never mind. I hand out cash. Whew. That was close.)

Sorry, distracted by lethal weapons. OK, here is the stage: President Trump, ah, my President and yours, has put the brakes on giving money to the WHO. Not the band, which has done, I believe, more farewell tours than the Rolling Stones, but the World Health Organization, or WHO. WHO is a part of NATO. NATO, the North Atlantic Treaty Organization, was formed in 1897 with Joe Biden as the U.S. signatory. Anyway, Joe was there and signed it, using the world's first-ever Bic pen. Joe was there with Chlodwig, Prince of Hohenlohe-Schillingsfürst, the Chancellor of Germany. Boy, they had stories to tell each other and hair to sniff. The chancellor noted that Joe's hair smelled like grease. Biden, a strapping 20-year-old replied, "Grease is the word, is the word, is the word."

Wow, outta my mind with distractions. Sorry. So, Trump is putting the brakes on WHO funding. The USA gives the most cash, with the wonderful couple, Bill and Melinda Gates, giving the second most money. These two folks, whatever their politics, should receive an even higher honor than what is currently available. We often say, "Put your money where your mouth is." Well, these two wonderful people do just that. Oh, if you are on a limited income and give five bucks to a worthy cause, like a food bank, you are JUST AS GOOD as the wonderful Gates, by the way.

Oh, Sweet Jesus Jason, get to the point. China lied. People died. Perhaps millions by the end of this. The WHO was like a fullback for China, blocking the way for their deception and deadly lies. The WHO's Director-General, a stupid man that threatened President Trump, leader of the country giving the most funding to the WHO, is, to this day, defending his malfeasance and sending out B.S. line after B.S. line. He is a rat trapped in a corner without the "cheese" that I suspect, was piling up in his bank account, thanks to the Chinese Communist "Let's Have A" Party.

Meanwhile (Scooby Doo segue), Democrat House Speaker Nancy "Liquid Nails for my Dentures" Pelosi is floating the idea of "impeaching" Trump again for his bitch-slap of the WHO. She claims it is Congress' role to determine world-wide relief and that the President has overstepped his authority. She argues that this is just like Trump's misdeeds with the Ukraine, which led to her failed impeachment of the President.

Really? Was Hunter Biden involved in China, like he was in the Ukraine? Oh, shit. Scratch that, he was. Never mind. The Dems have been on a mission: kill Trump with Maxine Waters calling for impeachment before Trump was even inaugurated; kill Trump with Stormy Daniels and Michael Avenatti; kill Trump with Russia, Russia, Russia; kill Trump with a Ukraine phone call; and now, kill Trump for calling to task a very corrupt international "health" organization that hid the severity of the Coronavirus while kowtowing to the even more corrupt Communist Chinese government.

As Michigan Dem Congressthing Rashida Tlaib said a couple of years ago, "Impeach the Motherf—ker!" Yes, please do, and put on the final shovel full on you grave, Dems! Americans will not put up with this political B.S. anymore.

MIA DURING THE CORONAVIRUS CRISIS: THE U.S. CONGRESS

A great friend of mine, a small business owner whose operations are currently on hiatus, his wonderful, talented and mostly young employees laid off, called me this morning with a simple question: "Why isn't Congress working?"

As many of you know, Congress is "off" (pun intended) until May 4th. "Why?" I responded, "I don't have a frickin clue, but I know that House Speaker Nancy Pelosi is busy making videos of her multi-gazillion dollar freezer packed with $13 a gallon ice cream."

OK, I got snarky there. My bad. But my friend's question is valid in this time of crisis. And, it is NOT a partisan issue: Republican or Democrat, why aren't you folks in D.C. doing your job? Note: Some will argue that when Congress is NOT working, less harm is done to our country and its citizens. But that is a separate issue.

Oh, some may argue, if Congress was in session, we would have 435 Representatives and their staffs packed like sardines in the chamber, violating all Social Distancing guidelines. Maybe, but then couldn't they employ temporary, emergency measures to allow only one-third of the members in the chamber at any one time and have those not in the chamber on a closed-circuit system to take part in any debate or proposed legislation? Hell, the IRS and the Treasury have the daunting task of efficiently getting relief checks to 70 million homes and bank accounts in all 50 states, and these clowns can't figure out how to run a session differently than in the past?

The same goes for the U.S. Senate and their 100 members, where a modified session would be even simpler.

But hold on Jason, they need to be home with their constituents, an important part of their jobs! At home to do what? Have an in-person town hall? Not now. Any town hall could easily be done on the Internet, with the legislator in his/ her D.C. office. Oh, here it is, they need to be able to visit infected constituents in their local hospitals. Ah, no, for the same reason given for in-person town halls.

I am all ears for legitimate reasons the two houses of Congress will not be in session for two more weeks. Feel free to chime in. Trump and Pence are working. Brix and Fauci are working. Heck, Guv Cuomo, when he is not talking about his mama's spaghetti and his daughter's boyfriend which he likes (He told us today during his crisis update briefing), is working, and very hard I might add, when he is not taking the occasional, snarky swipe at the President.

Why is this important? Tens of thousands of small businesses, the engine of our economy, are operating (or not operating at all) on FUMES! They need relief and only Congress can continue this relief…and can do it quickly. Or, they can just sit back, eat Haagen Dazs and bloviate on the Sunday TV Talk Shows, from their living room or hot tub.

Again, I welcome your opinions.

Christos Anesti!

CUOMO: DON'T LET MY PEOPLE GO!

Well, it's official: Americans SHOULD NOT protest overzealous clampdowns of the individual rights and liberties during the virus crisis. The word comes down from the Mt. Sinai Hospital mountaintop in the hands of Moses, ah, er, NY Governor Andrew Cuomo, who, this morning, said "there is no need to protest" to open up states now that the Coronavirus shows evidence of waning and before our national economy totally tanks.

These "bad, bad" protests have taken place in 23 states thus far, including Michigan where garden seed sales are banned at Home Depot and Lowes stores, and even The Republic of Maryland. Some protesters of the protests called the protesters TERRORISTS! (Say that fast three times.)

Of course, Cuomo and his ilk had absolutely no problem with thousands of women in Washington D.C. donning Pink Pussy Hats, protesting Trump even before he was inaugurated back in 2017. Heck, that was such a "proper" protest, especially when Like a Virgin Madonna jumped up on the main stage and said that she wanted to blow up the White House. Some would have called THAT a terrorist threat, but to the screaming Pink Pussy Hatters, it was music, in the moment, and vogue, vogue, vogue, vogue (fade out.)

But protesting a ban on buying garden seeds, fertilizer, lawn furniture, fishing, golf, visiting grandma or your elderly neighbor, and more should be off-limits, and as Cuomo COMMANDED, "unnecessary." Does the NY Guv have nine other Commandments to share with us? Maybe.

ANDREW CUOMO'S TEN COMMANDMENTS

1. Thou shall not protest "unnecessarily" as determined by him.
2. Thine state of New York budget shortfall will be an estimated $8 billion.
3. Verily I say, because the budget shortfall is ALL due to the virus crisis, the U.S. taxpayers MUST bail out the state.
4. Likewise, verily, there is NO TRUTH that the projected budget shortfall for NY this year was $6 billion BEFORE the virus crisis.
5. Thou shall never utter the financial numbers noted in Commandment No. 4 or they will be rounded up and prosecuted immediately after NYC Mayor DeBlasio finishes up jailing and fining anyone who does not follow Social Distancing Guidelines in the city.
6. Nowhere in the land of NY, shall a Chick-fil-A franchise apply for a small business loan relief check. Oh wait, Chick-A-fil, while delicious, is already persona non grata in NYC, and Chicago.
7. Thou shall not commit blasphemy like wearing a red "Make America Great Again" or "Keep America Great" and will be determined an act of domestic terrorism. NY citizens will not be prosecuted if they beat the holy snot out of any of these Nazis.
8. Thine Trump Tower in Manhattan will not be allowed to re-open until Hell freezes over.
9. Thouest Satan is a member of the Democratic National Committee steering committee and has assured us that he has plenty of charcoal in his reserves.
10. Alas, I sayeth unto all of you, once the virus is gone, I (Guv Cuomo) will not seek higher office, such as the Democratic nomination for President, no matter how much weaker a candidate Joe

Biden becomes as each day goes by. I will not replace Joe Biden on the ticket, despite my incredible accomplishments in the wake of this crisis, and certainly NOT because Joe Biden has some pretty nasty, and I must say, legitimate sexual harassment allegations against him; allegations that do not necessarily mean guilt, but look pretty darned ugly, and may result in a rape conviction unless he can squirm out of this one, which seems highly doubtful considering his diminishing mental state. Of course, I would be a much stronger candidate than Sleepy Joe: I can remember which state I am in, and, importantly, I call the current virus by its correct name, COVID-19, unlike Joe that calls it COVID-9. The "19" comes from the year it was first noticed, 2019. Perhaps there was a similar virus in 2009 when Joe was 87 years old, but I don't recall hearing about it. No, Joe is our guy, sink, swim or convicted.

FLY LITTLE JAIL BIRDY, FLY, FLY AWAY

More than 16,000 U.S. inmates in the hoosegow have been released into society due to the threat of Coronavirus. The states of New York and California lead the way, both freeing more than 1,000.

Why? Well, the standard answer is if they contract the virus, the state will have to pay for their treatment. Ah, but who pays if they get the virus after they're set free? Yep, probably taxpayers.

Of the two giant states, California seems to be the one that actually thought through a reasonable plan. The vast majority of freed inmates in California have been nonviolent criminals who were within 45-60 days of being paroled anyway. Smart move, in my opinion.

New York, on the other hand, has concocted a dog's breakfast of determining freedom. Most of the freed inmates were parole violators. Let me get this straight: so, some dude or dudette commits a crime, gets convicted, serves some time and is set free on parole. Then, that same dude/ dudette, on parole, commits another crime, and gets sent back to jail. Do you think freeing him/ her will mean they will walk the straight and narrow line THIS TIME?

But Jason, Jason, Jason, some of these folks probably did not commit another crime, they just missed a meeting with their probation officer, so no big deal. Sorry, that too is a crime, and if you are on probation after being jailed, you are probably up to no good if you can't find it in your busy schedule to obey the probation rules. It's not like probation meetings are every day. (Ah, not that I, um, er, know, uh, personally.)

Of course, in NY, it is not just about freeing parole violators. NYC Mayor Bill "Big Bird" DeBlasio actually freed a guy convicted of MURDERING an EMT, a first responder. Meanwhile, Big Bird is asking NYC citizens to rat on people not abiding by Social Distancing guidelines. Maybe he is freeing murderers to make room in the jail cells for those hideous and "violent" people standing to close together.

Now, while it seems like a mixed bag on releasing these criminals due to the virus, this could be a great opportunity for Michigan Governor Gretchen Whitmer to regain some of the early mojo she garnered in the crisis, but then sadly drained her credibility account with some bad decisions. Wait, they weren't "bad" decisions; they were stupid decisions.

So, here's my idea. Whitmer should let out all inmates convicted of robbery on the condition that they immediately hold up a Home Depot or Lowes or Menards – there are tons of them in the state – and steal all the garden seed packs and as much fertilizer that will fit in their recently stolen vehicle. Hopefully, they had enough sense to steal a Ram or Silverado pickup truck. Then, let them set up a roadside stand to sell their newly acquired bootie. The line-up of cars with eager buyers will be long. This is the very definition of a "two-fer." The citizens of the locale finally get the seeds and fertilizer they have been aching for, AND, the convicts get a "life skill" as an aspiring entrepreneur and will no longer need to sell crack and smack to make ends meet.

I'm a frickin' genius.

DEMOCRATIC OVERSIGHT OF THE CORONAVIRUS MONEY? HECK, LET'S GET FORMER DETROIT MAYOR KWAME KILPATRICK OUT OF THE HOOSEGOW AND PUT HIM IN CHARGE OF "OVERSIGHT"

Today, the Democrats in the U.S. House of Representatives voted along party lines (oh, they are back to work? I guess the ice cream binge is officially over. Sweet!) to create an "Oversight Committee" to "watch like a DEAD hawk on the side of the road" where the U.S. taxpayer dollars go to American citizens and businesses and Harvard University (oh, Harvard is giving back their $3 million grant when they realized their piggy bank couldn't fit another penny without "breaking.") You remember as a kid: "Mommy, mommy, my piggy bank is full; let's break it and go buy some candy!" So sad.

"Oversight" seems like a good idea on the surface when we are talking about billions, hell, maybe trillions of dollars when this all comes down. But let's go below the surface, courtesy of the Senate Appropriations Committee.

As the U.S. House is appropriating even more money for relief, much of it legitimate, let's look at some of the "essential' services which received millions of dollars in the prior bills, all shoved up the U.S. taxpayers' butts by the Democrats in Congress. I doubt there will be any "oversight" of these past gems.

The Corporation for Public Broadcasting got $75 million for "stabilization grants to maintain programming services and to preserve small and rural public telecommunication stations." My wife and I watch PBS once in a while, mostly their fairly lame cooking shows which pale in comparison to non-government cooking shows like Chopped and Diners, Drive-ins and Dives. But, the PBS stations in the realm of CPB need "stabilization." Does that mean they can bank the new $75 million and not subject us to their painful on-air begga-thons where if you give $25 you get a potholder and a Slim Whitman CD? If the answer is "yes," I am all for this ridiculous grant on top of the hundreds of millions a year they get normally.

The Institute for Museum and Library Services got a cool $50 million. For what? Ah, digital access and technical support services. What? They weren't doing this already? Crank up that lithograph machine, folks! I am certain this organization has been decimated, decimated I say, by the China virus, oops, Covid-19.

The Smithsonian Institution, a wonderful collection of museums by the way, hauled in $7.5 million for increased telework capabilities, deep cleaning of facilities, and overtime for security, medical staff, and zookeepers. Interestingly, all of the Smithsonian facilities are CLOSED! And, they are NOT losing revenues because attendance is free. Their online services have been in existence for years, so there is zero need for more funding.

Then, of course, there is the sloppiest pig whore of all this garbage: the Kennedy Center pocketed $25 million for "deep cleaning, increased teleworking capabilities, and operating and administrative expenses to ensure the Center will resume normal operations immediately upon reopening". Of course, seconds after getting this windfall of needless funding, the geniuses at the Kennedy Center laid off most of their staff. So, who is going to do the deep cleaning and other tasks noted in their grant?

But wait, it gets even sillier, if that is possible. The National Endowment for the Arts snared $75 million "for grants, including funding to state arts agencies and other partners in an effort to help local, state, and regional communities provide continued access to cultural organizations and institutions of learning." Aren't ALL of these local, state and regional facilities closed? Did they not have online programs prior to the virus? Did their Internet service fees increase due to the virus? Mine didn't.

So, will the U.S. House's "Oversight," led by the Democratic majority, look into these ridiculous appropriations? Don't count on it, one bit. However, if Speaker Nancy Pelosi tries to squeeze in an appropriation for the Institute for the Study of Really Expensive Ice Cream, I just might have an issue.

A HUGE TAXPAYER BAILOUT OF ILLINOIS? IT'S MUSIC TO THE DEMS' EARS

The State of Illinois' Democratic lawmakers are asking for more than $40 billion in "no-strings 'attached" aid from U.S. taxpayers. "Illinois could see an estimated revenue loss of $14.1 billion for 2020-2021 due to this (Coronavirus) pandemic," the Democratic leaders said in a letter to the Illinois congressional delegation earlier this month. "This loss would deplete approximately one-third of Illinois' general funds in one fiscal year, significantly impacting state services and long-term obligations."

The Coronavirus pandemic has no doubt put financial hardship on every state – just ask NY's Andrew Cuomo, but Illinois' projected need of $14.1 billion attributed to the pandemic seems like a long bumpy flight to the $40 billion they are demanding.

So, what makes up the remaining $25.9 billion hat-in-hand "request"? In two words, it can only be described as "financial malpractice," honed by the politicians in Illinois, much of it in Chicagoland, not for years, but for decades. Illinois' legendarily corrupt pension systems, as an example, are underfunded by at least $138 billion.

Here's what the Democratic lawmakers believe the U.S. taxpayers OWE the state:

• $15 billion in block grant funding to go directly into the state's coffers; and

• $10 billion in state pension relief.

Then, there is a need for $6 billion in unemployment trust funds because Illinois has one of the nation's lowest-funded unemployment trust accounts in the U.S. They are asking for a raise in federal medical help but didn't spell out how much they actually need. Then there is $1 billion in additional public health spending, beyond what they have already received from the Feds, in disproportionately impacted communities, citing the COVID-19 fatalities. Note: Illinois has 3.7 percent of the virus deaths in a population that consists of 3.9 percent of the total U.S. population. True, the vast majority of those deaths are, sadly, in Cook County, home of Chicago. This is at a time that New York and New Jersey account for 50 percent of the fatalities and nine percent of the total U.S. population.

The Democrats are also seeking $9.6 billion in aid for municipalities on the front lines of the fight against the pandemic, and "anticipate unbearable revenue losses as a result of the crisis."

So, let's add up the billions requested by the Democratic legislators from U.S. taxpayers: 14.1 plus 15, plus 10, plus 6, plus 1, plus 9.6.

That equals $55.7 billion they have spelled out, with, as noted, one request item with no specific funding. But they are asking for "only" $40 billion in their request letter. It seems that when the Illinois Dems want a bailout, like usual, even then they have a problem with basic math.

Who's to blame? The Virus? Yes, to some extent, but the real culprit is the financial malfeasance and corruption for which the state is infamous. Oh, and the fact that people have been fleeing the state for years due to ridiculously high taxes and an ever-decreasing return in actual services for which their taxes are collected.

They've got trouble my friends, right there in the Windy City (and the Land of Lincoln.)

Cue to the music, please. (My apologies to Meredith Wilson)

As Sung by Illinois Democratic State Senator Don Harmon
Illini Democrat leaders, we're either you're closing our eyes
To financial malfeasance and corruption we do not wish to acknowledge,
Or you are not aware of the caliber of disaster indicated
By the presence of a Pool of money we are requesting from U.S. taxpayers.
Well, we got trouble, Dem friends, right here.
I say, trouble, right here in the Windy City.
I'm certainly mighty proud to say,
Yes, mighty, mighty proud to say,
I consider that the hours I spend increasing taxes

With a gun at the head (of our citizens and businesses) are golden.
<u>Helps you cultivate a horse's ass sense,</u>
And a cold heart and a heavy wallet and a keen pallet for pork.

Now, friends, lemme tell you what I mean.
Ya got one, two, three, four, five, six pockets of debt we need to fill.
Pockets that mark the diff'rence
Between a gentleman politician and a loser Constituent,
With a capital "C,"
And that rhymes with "P" and that stands for a Pool 'o money!

And all Spring long in your Windy City
Youth'll be shelterin' in place
I say your young men'll be shelterin'
Shelterin' away their noontime, suppertime, chore time too!
Get the high score on a video game
But never mind getting' dandelions pulled,
Or the hair cut or the pavement pounded.
Never mind plantin' now seeds,
No WAIT, that's Michigan, yes indeed!
You'll shelter 'til your parents are caught with their bank account empty.

Yeah, we got trouble,
Right here in the Windy City.
Trouble with a capital "T"
And that rhymes with "B" and that stands for, egad, Bankruptcy!

Friends, an idle Democratic Illinois legislature is the devil's playground!

Trouble! Right here in the Land of Lincoln.
That's Trouble with a capital "T"
That rhymes with "B" and that stands for Bailout!

Remember the Maine, Plymouth Rock and the Golden Rule!
Oh, we got trouble,
We're in terrible, terrible trouble.
That political game of a Federal bailout is our only tool!

Oh yes we got trouble here! We've got big, big trouble!
With a capital "T"!
Gotta rhyme with "V"!
And that stands for Virus!

GET A CLUE: NOVEMBER PRESIDENTIAL ELECTION WILL HAPPEN

Several Democratic operatives and politicians are feverishly floating the idea that the Trump Administration, using the Coronavirus pandemic as an excuse, will DECLARE the November 3 Presidential election "delayed" or "canceled." It fits perfectly into their theory that Donald Trump wants to be King, not just President. Ah, this gives him the perfect opportunity. Hmmm.

These are the same Democrats that called for Trump's impeachment, even before he was inaugurated – thank you nutty Congressthing Maxine Waters. And, thank you equally nutty Congressman Al

Green, calling for Trump's impeachment, formally, three times on the House floor, the first weeks just after Trump took office.

In fact, on May 5, 2019, Mr. Green -- in his office, with a press release -- said that "if we don't impeach him (Trump), he will get re-elected." Get a CLUE, Al. I'd like to solve the case, although I was hoping it was VP Biden, with a finger, alongside the Capitol building.

So, let's see. President Trump wants to rip up the Constitution and declare himself a king – NO ELECTION FOR YOU, TWO YEARS!!!! The lawsuits would immediately overwhelm the Mesothelioma lawsuit commercials on T.V. and would make a beeline to SCOTUS. The ruling would be Nine-Zero against Trump: Actually eight-zero until Chief Justice Roberts nudges Ruth Bader Ginsburg to "wake up" and vote, "you're winning, Ruth. Push the 'yes' button."

Engaging the Way Back Machine, let's remember that back in 2008 through 2016, Democrats were constantly floating the idea that Republicans wanted to impeach President Obama. From what I remember, zero GOP operatives or politicians were calling for this. It was only Democrats that were screaming that the Republicans "wanted" to do this. Yes, yes, Senator Turkey Neck McConnell, did state early on that he wanted Obama to be a "one-term President," but there was NEVER talk of impeachment. It was a ruse parlayed by Democrats, period.

For the Democrats, I channel The Rolling Stones: "You can't always get what ya want. But you can try some time, ya get what ya need." But the Dems need Biden's gaffes and the Tara Reade sexual allegations to go away. To quote another '70s rock band, BTO: "You ain't seen nothing yet!"

DEFYING CHARITABLE WORK TO SAVE LIVES IN THE CORONAVIRUS CRISIS, GAY NYC COUNCILMAN PROVES HE'S A BIGOTED HORSE'S ASS

It's a modern-day example of the age-old axiom, "Don't bite the hand that feeds you." You know, don't look a gift-horse in the mouth.

According to various sources – OK, a guy at the Circle K down the street – the axiom is "somewhat" attributed to a 1700s British political writer, Edmund Burke, who later starred as Herman Munster in the '60s TV hit. No, that is not accurate.

The idea was "Don't criticize or hurt those you depend on; no matter long or short."

Fast-forward to modern-times New York City, I guess that axiom has fallen on deaf-or-thankless-even-ingrate ears.

Samaritan's Purse is an outreach of Franklin Graham's Christian ministry. Franklin is, of course, the son of the famous preacher Billy Graham. Samaritan's Purse has treated hundreds of COVID-19 patients at its field hospital in Central Park, New York City. They provided the field hospitals within days of the virus crisis on their own dime – if not millions of dollars.

But two days ago, NYC Council Speaker Corey Johnson demanded that the Christian charity leave the city over its biblical views on homosexuality. Bottom line: We hated you before this pandemic, we "put up with you when you provided relief," but, that is over. We hate you again. Get the effe out!"

"It is time for Samaritan's Purse to leave NYC. This group, led by the notoriously bigoted, hate-spewing Franklin Graham, came at a time when our city couldn't in good conscience turn away any offer of help. That time has passed," Johnson, the openly gay speaker wrote on Twitter Saturday. "Their continued presence here is an affront to our values of inclusion and is painful for all New Yorkers who care deeply about the LGBTQ community."

The Samaritan's Purse 68-bed field hospital has treated more than 300 patients since opening on April 1 in a city that became ground-zero of the Coronavirus suffering and deaths. Franklin Graham made it clear that their group's field hospitals would (and did) treat all patients and would not discriminate.

Said Graham, "while we lawfully hire staff who share our Christian beliefs, we do not discriminate in who we serve. We have provided billions of dollars (worldwide) of medical care and supplies, food and water, and emergency shelter without any conditions whatsoever. Our Christian faith compels us — like the biblical Good Samaritan — to love and serve everyone in need, regardless of their faith or background."

Well, it appears NYC Speaker Corey Johnson is NOT looking a gift horse in the mouth, as you cannot do that when, in fact, you are an unappreciative HORSE'S ASS! Unless, of course, you are a very, very flexible horse.

RUSSIAN COLLUSION HOAX REVEALED: FINALLY, AND HEADS WILL ROLL

Back in the summer of 1978 when I was 18, I bought a six-sing at the Five and Dime. No wait, that wasn't me. That summer I was living in Sweden, working at a factory that assembled and painted

Pella Windows. During the Midsummer holiday, I stayed on a lake island with my Swedish friend Magnus Fredriksson and a bunch of his friends.

On night while sitting around a fire, the conversation turned to American politics. The only American in the group, I talked about how embarrassed we were as a country with the whole Watergate scandal and Nixon's resignation four years earlier. One of the Swedes said something I will never forget: "Actually, you should be proud. It shows your system works. You get rid of the crooks."

Fast-forward to today and it appears that our system IS working again, and the crooks are on the run and some may soon find themselves in hotter water than Old Faithful.

The cover has been blown off the disgraceful, unlawful treatment of Lt. General Mike Flynn with his exoneration yesterday by the Justice Department. Yes, yes, I know that partisan, dishonest hacks like Congressthing Adam Schiff claim this is "by no means an exoneration" of Flynn. It is. Period. But it is so much more.

Multiple heads are going to roll very soon including two that sat at the top of the U.S. Intelligence Community under President Obama and lied under oath to Congress on multiple occasions – John Brennan and James Clapper. Also, in deep, deep trouble are other traitors in the rogue Obama Justice Department including lovers Peter Stroke and Lisa Page, Andrew McCabe and, hopefully, the liar and leaker himself, former FBI chief James Comey. Unfortunately, Adam Schiff will go unpunished, but hell, he has to live with his lying self, totally discredited and neutered. (Or, in his case, spayed.)

And one other big, fat liar may face the music.

It has been revealed in just-declassified congressional, behind-closed-doors testimony that former Obama administration defense official Evelyn Farkas testified under oath that she lied during an interview on Trump-hating MSNBC. In that interview, she claimed to have evidence of alleged collusion between the Trump team and Russia. But under oath, she admitted that no such evidence existed.

Grilled by then-Congressman Trey Gowdy, Farkas spilled the beans.

"…how did you know (about the Trump team colluding with the Russians)?" Gowdy asked Farkas.

"I didn't know anything," Farkas said.

"Did you have information connecting the Trump campaign to the hack of the DNC?" Gowdy asked.

"No," Farkas admitted.

"So, when you say, 'We knew,' the reality is you knew nothing," Gowdy asked.

"Correct," Farkas buicked.

"So, when you say 'knew,' what you really meant was felt?" Gowdy asked.

"Correct," Farkas burped.

"You didn't know anything?" Gowdy asked, sticking in the dagger one final time.

"That's correct," Farkas admitted.

Out of government, Farkas, a Democrat, is presently running for Congress in New York's 17th District. Good luck with that, girlfriend. She faces seven other Democratic candidates in a June 23 primary election. Hey Farkas, maybe you can have Adam Schiff campaign with you!

CHAPTER FOUR

THE SMITTEN MITTEN

MICHIGAN GUV GRETCHEN WHITMER: SOMETIMES YOU FEEL LIKE A NUT

As Americans across the country are housebound by the Coronavirus pandemic and there are real fears that some folks might get cabin fever and go wacko, Michigan, my former home and a state particularly hard hit by the virus, now has the designation of having the nuttiest, perhaps most dangerous governor.

Democrat Gretchen Whitmer seems to be doing her best to appear more like a dictator, soaking in news reports that she is a top pick to be Sleepy Joe Biden's VP running mate, and less like a leader solely interested in the citizens of the Mitten State.

Over the past few weeks during this pandemic, she has fumbled the ball more times than a Cincinnati Bengals running back. First, early in the crisis, she blasted President Trump for not providing needed medical supplies to the state, only to be told she was getting them ASAP, which came to fruition. Then, she banned the use of Hydro Chloroquine as a treatment for those with the virus, only to backtrack when success stories with the drug began to appear, including the miraculous recovery of a Democratic state congresswoman from Detroit who said she was on death's door before taking the drug.

Two strikes, but Whitmer wasn't out. Yet. (Sorry about mixing my sports analogies.) She banned visiting relatives and even next-door neighbors. That's right, if your elderly, disabled neighbor could use a hot bowl of chicken soup, you would need a catapult to fling the bowl from your house to her's, with the hope she had a big net to catch the hot bowl of goodness. Let's call that edict a "fowl" tip.

Oh, it gets nuttier, if that is possible. She "sort of" banned the sale of U.S. flags. Oh, you can buy Cheetos, Hostess HoHos, Vernors and Jack Daniels, but NOT Old Glory, at least not in a Home Depot or Lowe's garden center where they are on display. Millions of Americans could die if folks could buy a flag and fly it outside their house. Ahem.

And then, Whitmer did the Fonzie and completely jumped the shark: banning the sale of plant and vegetable seeds. What better way to perform social distancing than to get some radish seeds and going to your backyard garden – by yourself – and becoming an urban farmer. It good for both your soul and your salad. But NO!!!!! thanks to Great Leader, Gretchen Whitmer.

What's funny (as Andy Rooney used to say, "Not ha-ha funny, but weird or even sad, funny") is that Guv Whitmer has not banned the sale of another plant, weed, which is legal in Michigan. But, but, but, some will argue, marijuana is for medicinal purposes. Yes, for some, which is why it was first legalized in Michigan only for medicinal purposes.

By the way, it is "incredibly difficult" to get a medicinal marijuana card – you only had to go to a doctor and say, "I hurt…somewhere." But Michigan voters, realizing getting the card was as easy as getting herpes in a Detroit strip club on Eight Mile Road, said what the Hell, and made it legal for everyone -- those needing it for health reasons and those needing it to make it more comfortable when sitting on the coach in mommy's basement playing video games all day long, stopping only to open an envelope containing food stamps or an unemployment check.

Nor has Whitmer banned the sale of lottery tickets. True, you can buy lottery tickets online, but most still buy them standing in line, sometimes long when the Mega Millions or Power Ball is large, at a lottery outlet in a liquor store, gas station or grocery store. Of course, Whitmer actually is using a bit of logic with this twisted non-decision: the state reaps bigly sums of money from lottery sales. I guess she doesn't want to kill the goose that lays the golden egg, even if it means the virus is spread in the lottery lines.

Is it three strikes and you're out for a governor nuttier than Wuhan Chicken Salad? Well, a recall effort is underway as those disgusted with Whitmer are starting to plant the seeds for her removal. I wonder if she will ban those seeds as well.

Program Note: Who knows, maybe Whitmer is rethinking some of her bans and I missed something, although I searched dutifully on the Internet this morning. We shall see. If she does, I am afraid it will be too late to lose her title as the country's nuttiest governor. Good luck Uncle Joe if she is your pick, but be careful: she might ban hair sniffing.

GUV WHITMER DECLARES ABORTION A "LIFE-SUSTAINING" NECESSITY IN TOUGH TIMES

Yep, she said it. On the heels of ordering a state-wide ban on buying Home Depot or Lowe's garden seeds while hilariously keeping the cash cows of lottery ticket lines and marijuana dispensaries open during the Coronavirus pandemic, Michigan Governor Gretchen "Almond Joy" Whitmer has outdone her nutty self. I didn't think it was possible, but, alas, it is true.

Whitmer said that abortion is a "life-sustaining" procedure that must remain available during the Coronavirus pandemic. Repeat that sentence slowly. Rinse, repeat and hurl.

Many states have demanded that hospitals postpone elective surgeries during the pandemic. "We stopped elective surgeries in Michigan," Whitmer told former Clinton political operative David Axelrod on his podcast, The Axe Files. "Some people have tried to say that that type of procedure (abortion) is considered the same and that's ridiculous."

Ridiculous? Wow, I can't think of a more "elective" procedure than abortion, except in extreme and rare cases. Note: reviewing many online statistical reviews of abortions in this country, the generally agreed upon numbers are that 93 percent of abortions are for birth control, period, with the remaining seven percent due to a combination of rape, incest, health of the mother and serious health problems with the unborn child. According to Worldometers, there were 42.3 million abortions worldwide in 2019, the leading cause of death by far among humans. There is some good news. According to an NBC News report last year, the number of abortions per year in the U.S. is at the lowest level since abortion was legalized in 1973, down to "only" about 800,000 annually.

Back to Guv Whitmer's claim that calling abortion an elective procedure is "ridiculous." In the vast, vast majority of abortion cases, the pregnant woman "elects" to end her pregnancy, um, also called killing the unborn baby, or as some of the nuttier pro-abortion zealots call "it," a "collection of cells."

Well, Governor Whitmer, you sure have garnered the spotlight these days with your silly policies, but I think with this abortion stance, that spotlight has fried your brain and, sadly, your heart. Enjoy what is left of your first and only term in office. Oh, and your shot at becoming Joe Biden's pick to be his VP just got, well, aborted.

MICHIGAN DEMOCRATIC STATE LEGISLATORS "DISINFECT" THE GERM IN THEIR MIDST

Thank God for being prayerful and solemn in the midst of the Coronavirus, technically known as COVID-19 by medical experts and COVID-9 by Joe Biden. No better example of this reverence is happening now, in the Michigan State legislature. That august group is taking a vote to CENSURE Michigan state Representative Kate Whitsett, a Democrat from Detroit.

Her "crime or misdemeanor?" Did she misappropriate campaign funds for personal use? No. Did she engage in a sexual relationship with a staffer, or staffers, plural, both men and women? Nope. Oh, did she drive drunk and kill some folks in a car accident? Nada. Oh, I get it, she posted a threatening Tweet against someone! Ah, no. Again.

State Congresswoman Whitsett, not to be confused with Kate Winslet, the "selfish one" that laid on the floating door while Jack froze to death after the Titanic sunk – MOVE OVER AND LET LEONARDO GET OUT OF THE BONE-CHILLING WATER AND MOVE YOUR FAT ASS AND GIVE HIM SOME ROOM!! (The image still haunts me, but I WILL GO ON!)

Where was I? Damn! Anyway, Congresswoman Whitsett is facing a CENSURE vote today in the Michigan legislature via Skype. Censure is "to express severe disapproval of (someone or something), especially in a formal statement." (Thanks, Wikiwhatever for that definition.)

Her crime? She, get ahold of yourself now, THANKED the President of the United States for bringing attention to a "potential" drug to curb the Coronavirus, ah, COVID-19 or COVID-9. Number 9, Number 9. Congresswoman Whitsett was, in her own words, "on her death bed" after contracting the Chinese, oops, the Coronavirus, COVID-19, COVID-9, yada, yada, yada. She was on the verge of "buying the farm" and "going dirt up." And, stop it Jason, we get it! DEAD!

Congresswoman Whitsett, hearing about President Trump's praise of potential remedy, Hydro chloroquine, along with zinc, asked her doctor, obviously a person akin to Hannibal Lector, to give her the "controversial" 70-year-old medicine, used with great success on Lupus and malaria.

A few days after her Hydro Chloroquine treatment, the soon-to-be-six-feet-under Whitsett was peachy, swell, alive and well. Tragically, she, obviously in a state of both euphoria and DELUSION, went to the airwaves and proclaimed her magical recovery and her gratitude for the President of the United States – ah, those states include Michigan – and committed the greatest, most vile sin in the history of the Democratic Party – praising the evil Orange Man in the Oval Office.

Oh, the humanity! What a world! What a world!

So, today, for her transgressions, she will be spat upon by her colleagues – a scorned woman wearing the scarlet letters "DJT."

Said Congresswoman Whitsett, "I thought I had first amendment rights, but I guess I don't. The Democratic party is showing me that I don't."

Congresswoman Whitsett, welcome to TODAY's Democratic Party of hate, bitterness, hypocrisy and, as you sadly have discovered, cheap, hyper-political payback.

ESSENTIALLY DETERMINING "ESSENTIAL WORKERS" ACCORDING TO MICHIGAN GUV ALMOND JOY

Michigan Democratic Governor Gretchen "Almond Joy" Whitmer (sometimes you feel like a nut) on Wednesday announced a program modeled after the "post-World War II GI Bill that would provide tuition-free education for essential workers." Yes, the WWII "workers" were essential – ah, they were soldiers, like my Dad and his brothers, that saved the world -- and typically around 21 to 24 years old, battle-scarred, when they came home to America.

Her "Futures for Frontliners" program will apply to hospital and nursing home workers, as well as those working at still-open grocery stores, providing childcare, delivering supplies and manufacturing personal protective equipment (PPE), according to Whitmer's office. So, WHAT is an essential worker, Guv? Whitmer designated some, but with so many Democrat-inspired "feel-good" ideas, isn't it actually well-thought-out, if even thought-out?

Let's go in the WAY BACK Machine, shall we? Decades ago, led by the social-engineering geniuses, it was determined that the appropriate shitter, oh, excuse me, toilet, needed LESS THAN HALF of the precious water currently used to, um, er, flush. They, the environmentally conscious Einsteins came up with a plan forcing crapper companies, like Koehler, to make "better" toilets that used much less water. The result? They didn't – and don't work today. You need to flush sometimes three times to give Mr. Hanky his freedom down the porcelain poop chute.

Equally misplaced was the change to enviro-friendly light bulbs – replacing the normal one-dollar bulb with $9 bulbs that would save the planet. Only problem was/ is, when you drop one of Al Gore's magical "green" light bulbs, you need to hire a Haz-Mat crew to come into your home and keep your family from a Chernobyl event. It's an inconvenient truth.

So, here we are: Michigan Guv Whitmer trying to save her political life after early grandeur and then a long trip the last few weeks down a rat hole of stupid policies that have much of the Michigan folks up in arms. Literally – ah, stupidly -- and figuratively even today.

The free-tuition program, Whitmer's office said, aims to increase the number of working-age adults in the state with a college degree or technical certificate from 45 percent to 60 percent by the end of the decade. OK, on the surface, not a horrible idea, but two questions: who is going to pay for this program (ah, we know), but more importantly, WHO IS AN ESSENTIAL WORKER?

Whitmer lists doctors and nurses. They have degrees already, whether Med School or Nursing School or community college programs. So, I guess she might be pandering. Ya think?

Grocery workers, truck drivers in the supply chain? Swell. Firefighters, cops and EMTs? Sure, but let's admit, Guv Almond Joy is assuming, like most Dems do, that these folks are UNEDUCATED! Kinda sad, but typical among the ELITE policymakers.

But where do you begin to compile the LIST of ESSENTIAL WORKERS you want to give "free" education? Guv Whitmer, you list truck drivers supplying stores with goods, like food. What about the "traffic controller" directing which trucks get loaded and where they go? What about the dockworkers loading and unloading the trucks? What about the payroll people at these trucking companies that cut paychecks? What about the company's accountants and financial folks that make sure the money flows from customers to accounts payable to efficiently to keep the trucks rolling? What about the people that actually print the checks or send the money to direct deposit accounts?

What about the uniform and cleaning companies that provide clean hospital clothes and clean rugs for the hospital entrance ways? What about the stocker at Home Depot or Lowes that fills the shelves with tools for the construction trade and those hired to fix pipes and A/C so that folks' homes, where they are stuck, are livable?

What about the oil change jockeys at Jiffy Lube, or the car wash dude that keeps your car clean, so that the nasty viruses cannot attach to your car's hood and infiltrate your garage and home? What about the postal worker that continues to give you your mail and mails your packages?

OK, the list goes on and on. Where do you stop, Gretchen? How much will it cost? Importantly, if everyone is going back to school under your gracious and Nobel Peace Prize-worthy plan, who is left to provide these essential services?

Interestingly, when my family moved to D.C. back in the early '90s, soon we had a massive storm dropping two feet of snow that crippled our Nation's Capital. Early that morning, on radio and TV, was a warning that "non-essential workers" should not travel to work into the District.

I thought, what would you say if your kid asked you if you, Dad, were a non-essential worker. I thought about the potential conversation. "Dad, why aren't you at work?" "Well, son, I am NOT an essential worker." "Well then, you must be a LOSER, Dad."

Hey Guv Whitmer, I know that you are trying to get your MOJO back, but then think through it and don't shoot from the Lib, um, I mean the lip.

GUV WHITMER: METOO BACKS BIDEN; NO GARDEN SEEDS FOR YOU, MAYBE FOREVER!

For Michigan Governor Gretchen "Almond Joy" Whitmer, she has a new campaign slogan: "Out with the #MeToo; In with Restricting Free Speech and the Right of Free Assembly."

Appearing on ABC's *"The View,"* Whitmer threatened those Michiganders protesting her lockdown of the state -- if the protests do not end -- an even longer period than the current lockdown she already extended to the end of May.

"These protests, you know, in a perverse way, make it likelier that we're going to have to stay in a stay-home posture," she said.

Moments later on *"The View"* she added, "These have been really political rallies where people come with Confederate flags and Nazi symbolism and are calling for violence. This is not appropriate in a global pandemic but it's certainly not an exercise of democratic principles where we have free speech. This is calls to violence. This is racist and misogynistic."

No Governor. While those carrying legal weapons are stupid, and touting Confederate flags is abhorrent, both are legal in Michigan. By the way Guv, most, if not all of the Nazi symbols are targeted at YOU being a Nazi, not supporting the Fascists. Violence? You claim there is a "fear of violence," but that has not materialized, and all hope it doesn't. This is racist and misogynistic? How? Oh, you left off the protesters are "obviously" homophobic and Islamophobic, so you apparently lost a couple of pages from the Liberal song sheet.

Whitmer wasn't done. "While I respect people's right to dissent, they need to do it in a way that is responsible and does not put others at risk."

You respect dissent? Really? And so, you respect it by threatening your citizenry and stoke the fires even further? Please.

Also, on *"The View,"* Whitmer "officially" threw the #MeToo Movement in the trash bin.

Whitmer was an early front runner to be Joe Biden's pick as his running mate. While that chance has become more remote since a resounding backlash against her virus crisis policies, she remains a national co-chair of the Biden campaign.

When asked about the current allegation of sexual assault against Biden, Whitmer who claims she is a survivor of sexual assault, said she takes the allegation "very seriously," but still firmly supports the former VP.

"I take this very seriously. You know, as a survivor myself, I want you to know that women are able to come forward and to tell their stories and we listen to them. For a long time, women were dismissed," she said. "As a lawyer, I recognize that it's important that we vet and understand and ask questions and determine credibility of all parties in any type of an allegation."

So, how "seriously" is she taking the allegations?

"In looking at this, I think that the inconsistencies (what inconsistences, Guv??????) that I've seen gives me the judgment that I believe Joe. In this instance, I do believe Joe Biden, and everyone needs to make that judgment," she said, seriously. "The Joe Biden that I know is inconsistent with what we have seen and what we have heard around this particular allegation. I will continue to enthusiastically support Joe."

Ah yes, the "Joe Biden you know." #MeTooStillWantsToBeVice-President

MICHIGAN BE DAMMED! TRUMP PERSONA NON GRATA

Dam it! The State of Michigan is in a world of hurt these days. As if being one of the states hardest hit by the Coronavirus wasn't enough, the Mitten State received a double whammy this week when "bigly pouring" rains resulted in two dams along a major river failing, flooding millions in of acres Midland and surrounding areas. The 10,000 residents ordered to "stay-at-home" under Governor Gretchen Whitmer's controversial lockdown were forced to abandon their soggy homes and move in with relatives and friends on dry land. Dam, so much for the best-laid-plans of authoritarian leaders.

Now, Michigan needs some dam money on top of the Federal assistance they have received over the past couple of months to handle pandemic issues like ventilators, masks, testing equipment, etc. Initially, Governor Whitmer publicly complained about the Trump White House's slow response to the state's pandemic needs, but quickly played nice once the needed supplies started rolling into the state from the Feds.

While FEMA has already been on the ground, and quickly by the way, concerning the dam disaster, the needed financial aid may not be so easily and willingly forthcoming. Dam, why? A couple of reasons, both self-inflicted by Michigan state government officials, including the Governor, and Michigan environmental regulators. Let's take the latter issue first, shall we?

In 2018, Federal officials stripped the "license to operate" for one of the dams that failed this week and turned oversight over to Michigan state regulators. Those state officials then inspected the dam and its spillways and, channeling Kevin Bacon in "Animal House," declared "all is well." Actually, the term they used was "fair structural condition." It seems they had "bigger fish to fry," um, er, actually they were more concerned with the habitat of freshwater mussels in the dam area.

Michigan officials at the Department of Environment, Great Lakes, and Energy claim that regulators did not have enough time to do a dam-fine job of inspecting the dams before they gave way. Yep, they only had one-and-a-half years, even though the Feds had been warning the dam owners about "structural issues" for two dam decades.

Let's put that one-and-a-half years in perspective, campers. President Trump has been vilified, including by Michigan Governor Whitmer, for his initial "slow response" to the Coronavirus pandemic. Many Democrats have claimed, without facts, that the White House knew something big and bad was brewing in China two months before Team Trump "finally" acted in late January of this year. "Trump was told in December!" they shouted, despite the fact that in December and up until Trump's clampdown on travel from China on January 31st, the White House was being lied to by both the Chinese Communist Government and its Boy Friday, the World Health Organization (WHO).

Those two months of "delay" they claim resulted in "Trump" eventually killing thousands, if not tens of thousands of Americans. But, Michigan Governor Whitmer and her crack team, while ignoring the Feds stripping the dam owners of their license to operate and after decades of warnings, failed to do squat for the 18 months of her tenure. Two months versus 18 months: you be the judge of who was fiddling while Rome burned. Dam!

OK, OK, Whitmer was up to her eyeballs bludgeoning 77-year-old barbers who refused to obey her and stop cutting hair. She was also busy telling Michiganders not to travel to their up-north vacation cabins, although the latter edict did not apply to her family which continued to enjoy their lakeside home, three hours up the road from Lansing, as a get-away from all the noise of the pandemic. Interestingly, her family probably was driving through Midland in order to reach their Shangri-La in the woods. Not anymore though, thanks to the dam water.

Now, Whitmer is determined to prosecute those "responsible" for the dam disaster. Considering that a major suspect is Mother Nature's heavy rains which broke the dams' backs, I cannot wait for "Whitmer v. God" to reach the U.S. Supreme Court. It's not the Second Coming many of us were expecting, but it should be biblical. I can visualize Michigan Attorney General Dana Nessel telling the SCOTUS, "God, (didn't) dam it!" (More on that "mental giant" next.)

The other reason Federal financial help may be less-than-guaranteed for the dam problem all comes down to a senior state elected official, AG Nessel, having a big mouth, clearly visible despite the fact that her head is firmly planted in the southern hemisphere of her body.

Earlier this week, President Trump toured and spoke at a Ford Motor Company auto plant that had been converted to make much-needed (but not as much as Dem governors claimed, ahem) ventilators. Trump was there to thank the men and women of Ford for basically recreating the "Arsenal of Democracy" the automakers became during World War II when they turned their operations over to build tanks and Jeep vehicles. Ford Motor and its people were heroes then, and heroes now.

Michigan Attorney General Dana Nessel had warned the Commander-in-Chief in advance of the plant appearance that he MUST wear a mask while touring the facility and speaking to the workers. Trump took that "order" and basically said "Shove it!" although he did, in fact, wear a mask in certain intimate settings with Ford Chairman Bill Ford, viewing future cars Ford was working on.

Michigan political leaders lately have been very fond of ordering around both their citizens and, this week, the President of the United States. In fact, just yesterday Governor Whitmer extended her "stay-at-home" edict to June 12 after previous extensions, all of which have gotten a lot of Michiganders "hangry." Need a Snickers?

Almost immediately after Trump's appearance sans-mask at the Ford plant, AG Nessel publicly informed Trump that he was no longer welcome in Michigan after violating her "order," a day after the s—t hit the dam. Ve have vays of making you mask!"

Nice timing, Dana. Your "biting the hand that feeds you" qualifies you for a top job at the World Health Organization when this AG gig is over (mostly likely soon).

Here's what President Trump should do. Gather the much-needed dam financial aid Michigan will, without question, "demand," put it in the Presidential limo, and drive from D.C. to the Michigan border town of Toledo, Ohio. Open the trunk and show the gathered Michigan and national media the hundreds of millions of aid cash and then crank up the boogie box, playing M.C. Hammer's "Can't Touch This." He should replace his MAGA cap with one that reads, "The OTHER Michigan woman said I am not welcome in her state."

Dam! I guess the old saying about "loose lips" may result in those lips kissing Trump's keister in the near future.

MICHIGAN BOATGATE: GUV WHITMER IS RUDDERLESS!
PART TWO: THE GRAND ILLUSION

In yesterday's post (below) I noted that Michigan Governor Gretchen "Almond Joy" Whitmer's spokesperson, Tiffany Brown, in a statement said: "Our practice is not to discuss the governor's or her family's personal calendar/ schedules. And we're not going to make it a practice of addressing every rumor that is spread online. There's been a lot of wild misinformation spreading online attacking the governor and her family, and the threats of violence against her personally are downright dangerous."

It is apparent what was "downright dangerous" for the Governor in the Boatgate scandal was the clear and present danger to her sinking reputation. As I said, Whitmer had violated one of life's lessons: you cannot be a hard ass AND a hypocrite. Choose one or the other, but not both. It backfires on you.

Well, backfire it did, and so Guv Whitmer tossed away her spokesperson's pathetic dodge and decided to come clean. Check that: her acknowledgement that her husband had screwed the pooch was anything but clean. It was actually as or more pathetic than her spokesperson's earlier attempt to shrug off a claim of hypocrisy against the Governor's family, which was guilty on two occasions of violating her own "stay-at-home" edict, traveling to their northern Michigan vacation home.

Whitmer fessed up that her husband had requested the dry dock owner on the lake where they have a second home, put their boat in the water for use over the Memorial Day weekend. But, according to

Whitmer, her husband's efforts, including reminding the dock owner that he was "the husband of the Governor," thus entitled to special dispensation, was all a JOKE.

A little, harmless JOKE. Yeah, that's the ticket.

I think she is right. Her husband's hypocritical "do as I say, not as I do" antics, her spokesperson's phony dodge and, finally, her lame excuse ARE a joke.

Governor, your stand-up comedy routine just got the hook.

Here's yesterday's Boatgate post.

Michigan Governor Gretchen Whitmer is slowly and excruciatingly discovering some of life's lessons in her first and perhaps only term as leader of the Mitten State.

In the early stages of the Coronavirus pandemic, which has disproportionately impacted Michigan, she learned the lesson of "not biting the hand that feeds you." She had very publicly complained about President Trump's response to the growing pandemic at the very moment she needed a boatload (remember that term) of Federal government support, especially in terms of health care supplies the state was lacking. She got the aid the state needed, but not without some egg on her face.

But, I don't think she is close to learning the most recent life lesson shoved in her face: you can't be a hard ass AND a hypocrite.

Hard ass? Well, Whitmer wears as a badge of courage for the fact that her lockdown of the state's citizenry and businesses is arguably the most stringent in the country, right up there with loopy NYC Mayor deBlasio. Although she has relaxed some of her harshest edicts, partially due to a very vocal outcry among many of her residents, the memory of her folly will not be soon forgotten.

How harsh? She told Home Depot and Lowe's they had to close

their garden centers, the place where everything good for your spring planting is located – seeds, fertilizer, hoses, etc. She did this while allowing liquor stores and weed dispensaries to remain open. She said you couldn't visit your relatives or the old lady next door. And, she told Michiganders fortunate enough to have a second home or cabin in Michigan's gorgeous "up north" lake communities, to plant their butts in their primary homes in the southern half of the state and "stay there" and "shut up." No weekend retreat for you!

And just last week, Whitmer extended her "stay-at-home" incarceration for most Michiganders until June 12, AND while announcing restrictions would be lifted in some regions of Northern Michigan, she still urged, according to the ***Detroit News***, "those who didn't live in the region to stay away." "If you don't live in these regions... think long and hard before you take a trip into them," she said. "A small spike could put the hospital system in dire straits pretty quickly. That's precisely why we're asking everyone to continue doing their part. Don't descend on [waterfront] Traverse City from all regions of the state."

So where does the deadly combo of "hard ass and hypocrisy" come into play? Well, it "seems" that her "suggestion" not to "swarm" northern Michigan vacation hot spots like Traverse City – her vacation home is just 25 miles away -- did not apply to HER FAMILY.

It is reported but not concretely affirmed (more on that later) that the Governor's husband wanted to get the family boat out of dry storage to use on Burt Lake where their vacation home resides. He made the request a few days before the Memorial Day weekend. However, the dock owner told "the First Gentleman" that they were too backed up due to the previous lockdown to honor his request.

But the Governor's husband, Marc Mallory, wasn't taking no for an answer, at least initially. According to the dock owner, Tad Dowker, Mallory played the "do you know who I am" card saying, "I am the husband to the governor, will this make a difference?"

Apparently in his moment of desperation, Mallory had been hit by a "giant stupid stick." I can just imagine what was going through the dock owner's mind as he prepared to answer Mallory's "nod, nod, wink, wink, don't ya know" question. "Let's see, Mr. First Gentleman, would it make a difference? Would it make a difference? Well, you tell me, Einstein. Would it make a difference to you being in my shoes knowing your wife's authoritarian stranglehold on our economy has basically killed my business up to now?"

Mallory, reportedly, accepted the dock owner's denial of his request and the boat remained in storage, unable to christen the beautiful, clear waters of Burt Lake Memorial Day weekend. What a pity.

Now, I have said this incident was "reported by not concretely affirmed," first in the **Detroit News**. Why? Whitmer spokeswoman Tiffany Brown refused to comment specifically on the "alleged" Boatgate incident, saying the administration wouldn't address "every rumor that is spread online."

"Our practice is not to discuss the governor's or her family's personal calendar/ schedules. And, we're not going to make it a practice of addressing every rumor that is spread online. There's been a lot of wild misinformation spreading online attacking the governor and her family, and the threats of violence against her personally are downright dangerous," she said in a statement.

OK, I get it. I am certain that a boatload of Michiganders would like to see Whitmer dragged behind her family boat without any skis. But how about "addressing" THIS supposed rumor? It seems that this "rumor" has some teeth, also called a material witness. If I were the spokesperson I would most definitely address accusations that show my boss to be a flaming hypocrite at a time that she is under constant attack for being a hard ass, who is more concerned with snaring the

VP nod from Joe Biden than taking care of the cratering Michigan economy, and the livelihoods of millions of Michiganders.

Governor Whitmer, you can be a hard ass or a hypocrite, but you can't be both and get away with it. Otherwise, you rock the boat. Or is that dock the boat? Hmmm?

CONVICT KWAME KILPATRICK "AIN'T TO PROUD TO BAIL"

Should I stay or should I go? Thank you, The Clash.

I guess even the Coronavirus, despite its heinous impact on this country and the world, is not powerful enough to set a convicted high-profile felon free, 21 years before the chains of justice are scheduled to release him from bondage.

Former Democratic Detroit Mayor Kwame Kilpatrick, who was sentenced to 28 years in prison on corruption and fraud charges in 2013, will not be released to home confinement during the coronavirus pandemic, the federal Bureau of Prisons (BOP) said Tuesday, despite earlier "100 percent" claims from his supporters he was soon to be a "Free Bird."

Kilpatrick had plenty of people in fairly high positions promoting his early release – Michigan state Congresspeople Sherry Gay-Dagnogo and Karen Whitsett, as well as my old boss, former Compuware founder and CEO Peter Karmanos, who personally appealed to President Trump to release Kilpatrick from Louisiana's "white collar" Oakdale Prison.

None of Kilpatrick's supporters actually brought forth any evidence Kilpatrick was innocent of the crimes for which he was convicted. It was all about the nebulous notion of "fairness."

But "fairness" aside, Kilpatrick, who was convicted of fleecing the citizens of then-bankrupt and starving Detroit, came up with a "better plan" to spring himself from the hoosegow: The Coronavirus. After all, his cellmate, a 47-year-old man had died from the virus last month. Kilpatrick had escaped the deadly scourge, but the death was close enough for him to ask for freedom from his prison cell and a wonderful life of "house arrest" in his mother's home.

However, late Tuesday, the BOP denied the claim, according to the ***Detroit Free Press***.

"On Tuesday, May 26, 2020, the federal Bureau of Prisons reviewed and denied inmate Kwame Kilpatrick for home confinement. Mr. Kilpatrick remains incarcerated at the federal correctional institution in Oakdale, Louisiana," the BOP said in a statement.

Congresswomen Gay-Dagnogo and Whitsett said Trump had personally assured Kilpatrick would be released.

"I'm very disappointed and want to know why a sitting president would lie," Gay-Dagnogo said, according to the ***Free Press***.

Wow, it took ten paragraphs, but we finally got to the heart of the matter: It's Trump's fault. As we investigate the whole Kwame Kilpatrick crime scheme, we will undoubtedly discover that then-citizen Donald J. Trump had SOMETHING to do with Kilpatrick's malfeasance. Trust me.

There was hope for Kilpatrick. Attorney General William Barr in April ordered federal prisons experiencing Coronavirus outbreaks to release as many prisoners as possible to home confinement. Initially, it looked promising for Kilpatrick after eight prisoners in his prison facility had died of the virus at last count. But, in the end, the only thing dead for Kilpatrick was his freedom and life on mommy's couch.

Just to state the record: Kilpatrick, mayor of Detroit from 2002 to

2008, wasn't given a prison cell for a simple pot possession conviction: he was convicted of perjury, obstruction of justice, wire fraud, racketeering and mail fraud. If he is a model prisoner, he could get out in 2037.

I had "served" as a volunteer PR consultant to Kilpatrick. Early in his mayoral tenure, when the then-minor scandals started to mount, my boss at Chrysler, CEO Dieter Zetsche, asked me to give the mayor some strategic PR advice. I sat with the mayor for what I thought was a great meeting. I guess, in the end, he either ignored my advice or I sucked. The scandals soon began to overwhelm his reign until his resignation and imprisonment.

Key note: Kwame Kilpatrick, to this day, has not taken responsibility for his crimes nor shown a shred of remorse.

I think we all hope the Coronavirus is in our rearview mirror by his planned release date in 2037. In the meantime, Kilpatrick's mom should buy some of those plastic sofa covers to keep his future resting place fresh.

CHAPTER FIVE

SOME CONSERVATIVES GO FULL STUPID

"INEXCUSABLE! THESE CONFEDERATE FLAG & SWASTIKA-WAVING HOOLIGANS DEFY THE CROWN AND SPREAD DISEASE BY NOT SOCIAL DISTANCING!"

A MESSAGE TO THE FEW, THE PROUD, THE STUPID IN MICHIGAN

DISCLAIMER: I realize that the term "retard" is so, so politically incorrect. Sure, the generations after me, I think two gens actually, loved the term "retarded" -- "oh, my gawd, that's retarded, sha" -- and used it all the time when they weren't saying EVERYHING was "amazing!"

Of course, Harvard University's classic gridiron root for decades was "Retard them, retard them, make them relinquish the ball!" Funny, with that limp cheer it is no wonder Harvard football couldn't beat a 7th grade flag football team all those years. Oh, sorry, they beat Yale, once.

Alright, back to the issue, the WORD at hand: RETARDED.

If you have ever worked with these folks – the mentally challenged, whatever you want to call them – it actually gives you great purpose in your life, sometimes temporarily and sometimes long term. I have had and I have great friends in my hometown of Pella, Iowa that do it every day. People that help these "gifted folks" are treasures of humanity.

OK, enough of this schmaltzy crap. And, I am jumping off my political positioning and being supremely politically incorrect. Here goes.

My conservative "peeps" protesting in my old home state of Michigan regarding the shutdown of our society WHILE ARMED WITH WEAPONS are (pause) RETARDED!

Hello? You weapon-wielding dumbasses have feet to march. You have a voice to yell. You have the right to vote.

BUT, here is a point in time you need to remove your head from the southern hemisphere of your body. You DO NOT need to bring a gun to the protest!!! What? To shoot someone? To defend yourself? Against what? A renegade Lansing squirrel so bitter he couldn't eat leftovers from a Spartans football tailgate that Mr. Squirrel is paranoid he may never have that joy again?

Dear Michigan Conservatives: The incumbent governor is a colossal wreck. Keep your vehicle back from the accident clearly in front of you. If you can, pull off to the side of the political road and turn off the engine. Let the authorities figure out the massive pile-up on the highway your idiot Governor has created. And, check your stupid weapon.

NORTH OF THE SOUTHERN BORDER: A MEXICAN STANDOFF IN MICHIGAN!

"Pointless, inconclusive and unproductive." That's what they call the "Mexican Standoff" between Michigan Governor Gretchen "Almond Joy" Whitmer and her "Open Up the State Now! Dammit" opponents. She, Whitmer, the CEO of the Mitten State, wants to EXTEND the shutdown of businesses, the stay-at-home order, beyond May 15th; BEYOND the legally allowed time frame she was allowed to proclaim as Governor.

But, the Governor, a few weeks ago the "darling of the Dem Party and a sure-fire-bet" to be Finger Puppet Joe Biden's VP choice until she hit a speed bump that would break all the axles on a Mack truck, stepped, repeatedly on her, um, er, her authority. (Hey! Give me a break: At least "authority" kind of rhymes with "Johnson.")

This week, "that Woman," Whitmer, as President Trump once

dissed her, decided that she had enough of public discourse – ah, her citizens' voices -- and basically established "Martial Law" in Michigan, subjecting Michiganders to "Her Will." SO, LET IT BE WRITTEN, SO LET IT BE DONE!

Interestingly, on the FEDERAL level, ONLY the President of the United States can establish Martial Law. However, big however, Martial Law CAN be established by State Governors. So, Guv Almond Joy has an out for her supposedly "strong arm" tactics.

Of course, the "other side" of this "Mexican Standoff" is not silent. No, they are very vocal and active. Sadly, a few of the thousands protesting Guv Almond Joy are brain-dead morons that do not get, for a second, that rushing the Capitol Building in Lansing, ARMED, makes them look like psycho mouth-breathers. Trust me, 99.9 percent of my conservative friends, while never wishing evil on anyone, hope these brain-dead dorks soon find a man-killing giant Asian carp sucking on their neck as they bleed to death in their swamp boat, near their trailer, down by the river."

Oh, crap, I need to floss. Sorry.

Finally, for the life of me, I cannot find an actual source that says the term "Mexican Standoff" is a racist term. If anyone is offended, please tell me why, other than, "I just feel offended."

CHAPTER SIX

AS SEEN, BUT NOT TO BE BELIEVED, ON T.V. AND THE INTERNET

CNN'S CHRIS CUOMO: FAKE AT LAST! FAKE AT LAST! THANK GOD ALMIGHTY HE IS FAKE AT LAST!

While President Trump regularly accuses CNN of broadcasting FAKE NEWS, it seems the struggling cable giant has outdone itself this time, and the star of the fakery is none other than CNN's "golden boy" anchor, Chris Cuomo.

As you probably know, the brother of NY Governor Andrew "I love my mama's spaghetti and my daughter's new boyfriend" Cuomo and the leader of CNN's daily Trump hit squad, which includes Don Lemon and Brian Stelter, contracted the Coronavirus in late March – or at least he said he did.

Being the hero and great family man he is, Cuomo immediately self-quarantined ALONE in his basement and began broadcasting his show from there via Skype. Alone was this hero as to not infect his wife and children. What a guy, what a role model. Oh, almost forgot, in his basement broadcasts, Cuomo regularly chided people that were violating the stay-at-home guidelines for those infected.

Then, with great fanfare, on April 13, as the CNN cameras rolled, Cuomo walked up a flight of stairs, full of emotion about how grateful he was to finally get out of that basement and see his loving family! As I watched, tears flowed, and it immediately reminded me of when "Lassie came home" to little Timmy.

Here's what Cuomo said as he looked into the CNN camera: "All right, here it is. The official reentry from the basement. This is what I've been dreaming of, literally, for weeks. This is the dream, just to be back up here, doing normal things".

Let's face it: it was much, much more emotional than when the American hostages escaped from Iran back in 1980 after 444 days of sheer hell, not knowing if they would survive the Ayatollah's wrath and the angry, blood-thirsty mobs. But (there is almost always a but, and this one is a YUGE but), the world would soon learn that Cuomo had already "escaped," THE DAY BEFORE! Ahem.

It seems that while Cuomo was staring certain death in the face, he decided on Easter Sunday, the day before his "official" famous "re-entry," that he miraculously healed "thyself" and was strong enough to reemerge from his basement confinement, grab the wife and kiddies and pile into a vehicle for a 30-minute trip to the Hamptons to check on his property where he plans to build a new house. Now, I don't know what vehicle Cuomo took to the Hamptons, but unless it was a school bus, his family was confined in close quarters on the ride there and back.

None of this would have been known, but Cuomo, while on his Hamptons lot, decided it was the perfect time to get into a verbal altercation with a 60-something local riding by on a "fat-tire" bike. From the sounds of it, it was actually more of a Cuomo temper tantrum than an altercation. The bicyclist apparently had the audacity and the nerve to question why the famous Cuomo, supposedly in self-quarantine with the virus, was up and about, and outside with his family, miles from his home. After the ordeal, the "old man on the fat-tire bike" filed a complaint with the local police.

Perhaps even dumber, after returning home, Cuomo was interviewed by a radio program where he bitched and moaned about people, like the bicyclist, that could harass (really?) him and that his high-profile (and ridiculously high-income) prevented him from telling them to go to hell. Ah, Chris, don't you remember a few weeks ago you had another verbal altercation with a NYer who called you "Fredo" (aka, Michael Corleone's stupid older brother) and you threw out more F-bombs than Andrew Dice Clay, and threatened to throw the guy down the stairwell. Remember?

CNN, ever the purveyor of THE UNBIASED TRUTH, of course played along with Cuomo's fake "reemergence" the next day with great fanfare. To them, it was "must-see TV." Too bad it was 100 percent contrived, and FAKE!

Oh, the next day, Tuesday, Cuomo's wife came down with the Coronavirus and his son a few days later. I guess CNN's hero turned into a goat...a lying goat.

LARRY KING LIES?

Did Joe Biden or his campaign have a finger, I mean a hand, in making the now infamous August 11, 1993 episode of *"Larry King Live,"* reportedly with Tara Reade's mother calling the host, suddenly disappear?

Reade is the former Biden Senate staffer who claimed decades ago that Biden had sexually assaulted her while under his "tutelage" and earlier this month filed an actual charge with the police in D.C. Interestingly, *The New York Times*, *The Washington Post* and CNN refused to carry the latter until forced to after two weeks of holding out. Why? Well, you be the judge.

Yesterday, the story got, depending on your take, weirder or scarier, or perhaps even criminal. That particular episode, from 1993, was inexplicably REMOVED from Google's Playlist of the talk show host's hundreds of episodes on file for your viewing. The episode before the fateful August 11 show is there, as is the August 12 episode. But the August 11 episode, which gives substantial credence to Tara Reade's accusation against Biden has gone POOF, 86ed, s—tcanned!

J.L. Hamilton (@absinthol) yesterday tweeted: "CNN removed the August 11th, 1993 Larry King Episode from Google Play, the episode featuring a call from Tara Reade's mother. CNN is actively colluding with the Biden campaign to cover up evidence of Biden's sexual assault. pic.twitter.com/JqTcofIyqs"

If that is true, CNN's lack of coverage of Reade's recent police filing goes beyond sad and exposes clear collusion between CNN and the Biden campaign. Yes, yes, I know CNN hates President Trump and wants Biden, to win in the worst way; but this is even "worse" than the worst way. What makes matters worse for the cable network that features Trump-haters Chris Cuomo, Don Lemon and Brian Stelter, is that Larry King Live was a CNN-produced and aired show. And, by the way, CNN did not bring the now infamous LKL episode to light: it was either NewsBusters or the Media Research Center.

CNN obviously doesn't know what is in their archives. Or, maybe they absolutely do.

CNN is trying to defend itself of any dirty political tricks, claiming the network "doesn't have a distribution deal with Google Play. What they (Google) display in their catalog about Larry King Live didn't come from CNN, so Google controls whatever is displayed there."

But that claim does not negate the fact that CNN DID NOT unearth the damning video – ITS damning video potentially implicating Biden. No, that took outside sources. Again, let's remember that CNN refused to put the Reade allegations on the air until seemingly forced to weeks after the story broke. Making matters perhaps even scarier is that after the Reade allegation and police filing came to light, CNN's "investigative journalist supreme" Anderson Cooper, interviewed Joe Biden TWICE, yet never once asked 'ol Finger Puppet Joe about the allegation.

As Rocky Balboa told Mick in the first Rocky movie, "it stinks!"

I suspect that today, Google and CNN will get into a "Who Killed J.R." pissing match. Should be fun. No, not fun. Scary, if either, or both, had a hand or a finger in this alleged deception.

Stay tuned.

GOOGLE, YOUTUBE AND FREE SPEECH: ANOTHER ONE BITES THE DUST!

If you go onto Google's YouTube, you can easily find a video of Dr. Zeke Emmanuel claiming, on MSNBC, that it will take 18 months for the U.S. to come back to "normal." His appearance was in early April. The video is still up and running on YouTube. Emmanuel, in the video, offered little, if any scientific or statistical analysis to back his claim, no matter how scary it was.

Emmanuel, you may remember, is one of the architects of Obamacare along with fellow "architect" Michael Gruber, professor of economics at MIT; the latter who admitted in a taped presentation that Americans were lied to about the new health care plan in order to get it through Congress and signed by President Obama. In fact, on December 13, 2013, Politifact labeled Obamacare's "If you like your doctor, you can keep your doctor," the "Lie of the Year."

And, of course, Dr. Zeke is the brother of former Obama top staffer Rahm Emmanuel, who infamously said, "Never let a crisis go to waste."

Apparently, Dr. Zeke took his brother's advice, and wasted no time throwing gasoline on the Coronavirus fire.

Again, Dr. Zeke's video is STILL on Google's YouTube. Yes, that

Google: the folks that apparently removed from its playlist the now juicy 1993 Larry King Live interview of who is believed to be Tara Reade's mother, talking about bad behavior against her Senate staff daughter by a prominent U.S. Senator. Mrs. Reade's daughter, earlier this month, filed a sexual assault charge against former Senator and V.P. Joe Biden. The younger Reade also has several corroborators to her assault allegation that have come forward.

Regardless, the Google playlist of hundreds of "*Larry King Live*" episodes no longer includes that August 11, 1993 episode, presumably with Tara's mom. It went poof on Google's site, although you can still find it on other websites.

Yesterday, Google's YouTube decided to take down a video, initially broadcast on a local television station in California, that went viral attracting more than 4.3 million views in short order. The video, by doctors Erickson and Massihi, over the course of around 20 minutes, lay out "their science and statistics" to support their opinion as practicing physicians that the hype over the Coronavirus, and the current steps to shut down the country, are overwrought. Heck, they even conclude the actions that continue today with some "folks," supposed experts, claiming we are more than 18 months away from "returning to normal," (See Dr. Zeke above), are more dangerous than the virus itself.

My wife and I watched the video, all of it. I am no doctor, but as an economist in the early stages of my career – like AOC, I have an economics degree, but thankfully, I think I know how to use it, including understanding statistical analysis and kindergarten math – I found the doctors' analysis both compelling and thought-provoking. Could they be "all wet?" Maybe, but it is their educated and researched opinion. And many of their conclusions fall directly in-line with other studies done at Stanford University and by Japanese scientists in China.

I "assume" Dr. Zeke's opinion was equally educated and researched, although I have my doubts, just as people are free to have their doubts about the opinions, research and conclusions of the two California doctors on the now-famous video – a video that Google's YouTube has nixed from their site. For the "fair-minded and totally unbiased Google" it is two strikes of censorship within the matter of a week.

Apart from the video being taken down, it seems, as Jimmy Durante once said, "Everybody wants to get into the act." The American College of Emergency Physicians (ACEP) and the American Academy of Emergency Medicine (AAEM) released a joint statement which accused the California doctors of "attention-seeking to further their careers." But those two renowned organizations didn't actually refute the arguments in the now s—tcanned video.

Ari Allyn-Feuer, an Artificial Intelligence engineer at a major pharmaceutical company, and holder of a Ph.D. in Bioinformatics from the University of Michigan, with studies in Math and Biology at the University of Chicago, in a piece yesterday, attempts to tear down the California doctors' analysis, and encourages those interested to follow him and read his views on the video. However, in his piece, he asks a great question: "Whether they (the California doctors) prove to be right or wrong, whether you agree or disagree with their theories or political opinions, is there anything in the video that justifies banning it or undermining free speech?"

The answer, Dr. Allyn-Feuer, is an unequivocal NO! Unless, of course, you are the Google and YouTube "Speech Gestapo."

CNN INTIMATES TRUMP LYING ABOUT SEEING CORONAVIRUS ORIGINS EVIDENCE AND LACKS BASIC READING SKILLS

It was a blaring CNN Politics headline in the Google feed on my smartphone: "Trump contradicts US intel community by claiming he's seen evidence coronavirus originated in Chinese lab." Only problem is, the actual article doesn't say anything close to that.

But, of course, for CNN, it's their set-in-stone formula: Intel Community = Good; Trump = Bad.

The actual CNN story below the incendiary headline? Here's the skinny. The Intel Community put out a statement yesterday that said it was "exploring" two possibilities for the origins of the Coronavirus -- the infamous Wuhan lab and infection from an animal -- but had not reached a conclusion. Yet. Importantly, the Intel Community DID NOT say they had NO EVIDENCE regarding either possibility. In that regard, they "demurred." Remember that word, demurred. It's French for "punted," I think, sorta.

Hours later, President Trump "supposedly," according to CNN, "contradicted" the Intel statement, saying that he had seen "evidence" the gives him a "high degree of confidence" the coronavirus originated in the Wuhan lab.

Am I splitting hairs here? No. Again, the Intel Community said it is exploring two options and have not reached a conclusion. But they did not say what evidence they have thus far compiled.

When Trump was challenged as to what "evidence" he had seen, CNN referred to his response as "the President demurred." No, he didn't demur. In CNN's own article, they quote the President saying,

"I can't tell you that. I am not allowed to." That's not demurring; it's stating a fact. If he had truly "demurred," he would have said, "I'm not going to tell you," with no explanation.

Again, Intel Community is good, Trump is Bad. The hallowed Intel Community Spies, and Trump Lies.

Remember now that this "Intel Community" was once led by James Clapper and John Brennan, both who lied under oath to Congress on more than one occasion. It's interesting that both liars have become paid contributors to Trump's most fierce enemies in the cable sphere: Clapper with CNN and Brennan with MSNBC.

Back to the article. Near the end, CNN then went on a tangent saying, according to an unnamed Intelligence official (convenient, huh?), "Trump does not spend much time pouring through the daily (intelligence) briefs. Instead the President prefers intelligence officials to present him with policy ideas, rather than raw information… He doesn't like information, he likes decision points."

Let me translate that "World According to CNN" nugget: Trump is stupid, can't read more than a sentence and is trigger-happy.

Well, in my experience, CEOs expect that the investigating person / team did their research, explored all relevant avenues and came to him / her to make a DECISION. That is the way smart and efficient operations run. But to CNN, it is further evidence that Trump is BAD and now, careless and stupid.

The last two descriptors – careless and stupid – seem to apply perfectly to the Trump-hating cable network. Oh, and biased. But boy, their headline writers sure know how to stoke the "gotcha" fire.

JIMMY KIMMEL: THE LYIN' KING

For years now, there has been a saying in Washington, D.C.: "The most dangerous place on earth is the space between a television news camera and (Senator) Chuck Schumer."

Now there is a new saying: the most difficult thing to get out of a Liberal is a real apology when they are clearly busted for making up stuff in order to damage someone they don't like.

Case-in-point for this new saying is ABC late-night talk show host Jimmy Kimmel. This past Thursday Kimmel took a shot at Vice President Mike Pence, showing him supposedly carrying empty boxes of PPEs for a "publicity stunt" at a nursing home in Virginia. During his Thursday night broadcast, Kimmel mocked the vice president over the press event, which showed a mask-less Pence helping other workers deliver PPEs from FEMA to the front of the facility. As the video of Pence, played, smart-ass Kimmel said, "Here he (Pence) is, with no mask on, wheeling boxes of PPEs into a healthcare center, and doing his best to lift them. What a hero."

Oh, Kimmel wasn't done. He intimated that Pence stupidly didn't realize his mic was still "hot" as he talked to another official standing alongside the van that contained the boxes of PPEs. The official mentioned to Pence that the boxes in the van were empty, to which Pence quipped, "Well, can I carry the empty ones, just for the camera?"

At that point, Kimmel's crack production team cut off the video, but Kimmel continued his dissing of Pence, saying, "Mike Pence pretending to carry empty PPEs into a hospital is the perfect metaphor for who he is and what he's doing: a big box of nothing delivering another box of nothing."

There was a little, bitty problem with what Kimmel was showing and saying to his late-night audience. When the full, unedited C-SPAN video saw the light of day, it showed Pence actually delivering boxes FULL of PPEs, and later, JOKING, that's right, JOKING about the empty boxes, saying "they're a lot easier."

The joke, in the end, was on Kimmel. When Kimmel's team was told of their BS editing of the video to portray something it was not, the show quickly took down their Tweet highlighting their bogus treatment of Pence.

It was time for Kimmel to apologize to the Vice President of the United States. Did it go something like this: "The other night we showed a video of VP Mike Pence, and we unfairly edited it to make it look like Mr. Pence had done something that he actually didn't do. I apologize on behalf of myself and our show?"

The answer is NO!

Instead, little Jimmy tweeted the following: "It would appear that @vp was joking about carrying empty boxes for a staged publicity stunt. The full video reveals that he was carrying full boxes for a staged publicity stunt. My apologies. I know how dearly this administration values truth."

What a putz.

CENSORSHIP AND A BIASED MEDIA: THE HITS JUST KEEP ON A COMIN'!

The Liberal media are a bloc of some of the most anti-gun folks on the planet, oftentimes mislabeling guns as "assault weapons," when they are merely rifles, or going so far as to calling single-firing guns "fully automatic" weapons. I'm not here to argue gun rights, as

I really don't have a dog in the fight. But it seems like, these days, the media is constantly SHOOTING itself in the foot, further discrediting their trustworthiness and adding to charges of extreme bias.

We saw it a few weeks ago, when Google withdrew from their online files an episode of "***Larry King Live***" from 1993, that appeared to implicate Joe Biden in the Tara Reade sexual assault case. A week later, adding insult to injury, Google's YouTube nixed a video showing two California doctors taking issue with the current shutdowns throughout the country due to the Coronavirus. The latter, first shown on a California TV station, had garnered almost five million views on the Internet and was too much "free speech" for the "pandemic experts" at YouTube.

The latest episode, of what can only be called "censorship," involves NBC News, and its "***Meet the Press***" anchor Chuck Todd. It is no secret that ol' Chuck does not care much for President Trump nor his Administration. I'm being nice here. Besides CNN's Jim Acosta, Todd is probably the snarkiest "newsman" in MSM.

Well, Sunday, May 10th, Todd took his snarkiness to a new level: fraudulent reporting. A flim-flam. Todd played a video clip borrowed from CBS News in which Catherine Herridge, days earlier, interviewed U.S. Attorney General William Barr about the Justice Department's decision not to pursue criminal charges against former National Security Advisor Gen. Michael Flynn. In the interview, Herridge asked Barr how he thought history would remember last week's Flynn decision.

Without hesitating Barr answered, "Well, history's written by the winners. So, it largely depends on who's writing the history."

Barr, of course, was not finished with his answer. But Chuck Todd was. That was all of a much longer video clip he and NBC would NOT show. Why? Simple: To deliver on the "promise" he made to his viewers earlier in the show when he told him to "wait until you hear the answer" from Barr.

So when the edited clip of Barr was played with the "history's written by winners" line, and then abruptly ended, Todd looked into the camera, smirked and said he was "struck" by its "cynicism." Todd wasn't done. Seconds later, he chastised the Attorney General, the nation's top law enforcement official, for not making "the case that he was upholding the rule of law. He was almost admitting that, yeah, this is a political job."

But there was one itsy, bitsy problem: in the full interview on CBS, Barr's VERY NEXT WORDS were that the Flynn decision "upheld the rule of law." Nor did Todd show Barr say that the decision "upheld the standards of the Department of Justice, and it UNDID WHAT WAS AN INJUSTICE." (My emphasis.)

NBC News issued an apology six hours after the broadcast, and as usual, it was half-hearted, saying that they had "inadvertently and inaccurately cut short a video clip." They also said they "regret the error." Not quite a "we're sorry," but with today's Trump-hating media, it was about as good as it gets, and a helluva lot better than sanctimonious Jimmy Kimmel's faux apology last week, after the "comedian's" phony video editing and dishonest swipes at Mike Pence, while the VP delivered PPEs to a retirement community.

As for an apology from Chuck Todd? Crickets.

LIBERAL CENSORSHIP ON STEROIDS

The censorship hits are coming faster and more frequent than renewed calls for President Trump's impeachment. This past Sunday, it was ChuckToddGate where the NBC News' "***Meet the Press***" anchorman rigged a video from another network to make Attorney General William Barr look like he was shirking his duty to uphold the "rule of law." Todd's deceptive work was soon busted, and NBC News apologized. Kind of. Todd did not.

These shenanigans followed censorship by Jimmy Kimmel, Google's YouTube concerning two California doctors questioning the effectiveness of the nationwide "shutdown", and later Google "magically" removing ONE "***Larry King Live***" episode from its exhaustive catalog of the talk show host's episodes. The ONE episode deleted, from 199 on file, just happened to back Tara Reade's accusation of alleged sexual assault at the "hands" of then-Senator Joe Biden.

And today, the beat goes on. On May 2nd, Twitter put a lock on the account of a conservative commentator. She just happens to be a Black conservative commentator – a "no-no" in the eyes of the Liberal media. Her name is Candace Owens. She has more than two million followers. On top of that, Owens is an "African American who is articulate and bright and clean…" Check that: that was a description of Presidential candidate Barack Obama back in February 2007, by his running mate, then-Senator Joe Biden.

Boy, despite being stuck in his Delaware basement, Biden is quickly becoming a part of every story these days.

Twitter, one of the "duly elected" members of the "speech police", suspended Owens after she posted a tweet criticizing Democratic Michigan Governor Gretchen "Almond Joy" Whitmer, calling her a "duly elected dictator," and encouraging Michiganders to "stand up" to Whitmer's highly controversial extended stay-at-home orders and go back to work and reopen businesses.

In the good 'ol days, if you were a Liberal, Owens' tweet would have been (and would be today) considered both Constitutionally-guaranteed free speech and civil disobedience. After all, Governor Whitmer had been called worse, and, as a matter of fact, had called protests against her worse. Owens, not once, called for violence of any kind.

However, in her tweet, Owens failed to encourage residents of the Mitten State to storm Home Depot and Lowe's garden centers and clean out the garden seed aisle. Surely, a lost opportunity on her part. Ahem.

It is not the first time the Speech Police at Twitter has thrown Owens into the Social Media Hoosegow. They locked her account two years ago for a short time.

Her "Twitter Crime" then? Owens had the audacity to take tweets from a New York Times editorial board member, Sarah Jeong, edited those tweets and then posted her edits.

Here was one of Jeong's "perfectly fine" Tweets: "White people are only fit to live underground like groveling goblins. They have stopped breeding, and will all go extinct soon. I enjoy being cruel to old white women." It was just one of many anti-white tweets by Jeong.

Sadly, the New York Times backed their board member.

To prove a point, Owens changed "white" to "black" and tweeted: "Black people are only fit to live underground like groveling goblins. They have stopped breeding, and will all go extinct soon. I enjoy being cruel to old black women."

Twitter locked Owen's account.

A few days later, the protests against Twitter were even too much for this Gestapo-like social media platform and Twitter apologized to Owens and unlocked her account. Owens responded to her "parole" by saying that she was "BLOWN AWAY by the amount of patriots that just came to my side to make this happen."

Owens was finally free to voice her opinion…in America.

Until May 2, 2020.

Her new "Twitter Prison Sentence" continues as we speak.

UPDATE! UPDATE! READ ALL ABOUT IT! CLAPPER LIES AGAIN!

Yesterday I shared the post below (Lying is Easy…) about proven liar James Clapper's pathetic appearance on CNN "trying" to explain "unmasking" and how he and his colleagues-in-potential-crime had done nothing wrong.

After that post appeared, I got an email from a dear friend who has worked in D.C. for decades, including within the Federal Government. He has a theory about this unmasking situation.

While the CNN anchor was coaching Clapper on his answers, he (the anchor) was correct when he said that the practice is legal, but it only becomes illegal when the unmasking, with classified information, is leaked to unapproved officials, like the media.

The Flynn unmasking WAS leaked to ***The Washington Post*** on or about January 12, 2017, a week after a White House meeting on the Flynn investigation, that included President Obama, VP Joe Biden, and others.

Here's my friend's theory. It starts with a question: Why did 16 members of President Obama's team, including a couple of U.S. Ambassadors completely unrelated to Russia, request and receive the unmasking of Flynn? His theory? There was a plan concocted to leak the information to the media, which happened. By having 16 different Obamaites request and receive the same unmasking of Flynn, it makes it that much more difficult to pin the tail on the donkey that broke the law. Hmmm.

Doesn't sound too far-fetched, does it? I do know one thing: they didn't leave it up to Joe Biden to "leak it." He would have mistaken the request as permission for him to take a potty break, and at his age, you DO NOT pass up potty breaks.

LYING IS EASY WHEN THE INTERVIEWER IS COACHING YOU

This morning I witnessed one of the most bizarre interviews I have ever seen. It involved noted liar James Clapper, a former top government spook, proven UNMASKER and current CNN paid contributor.

What is interesting is not that Clapper is obviously lying, but how the CNN interviewer was actually coaching Clapper on how to answer his questions. In fact, it was the anchor that was really providing the answers for Clapper within his questions.

I call it a "guided interview," where the interviewer has an agenda that he shares with the interviewee and just wants to make sure the interviewee doesn't screw it up with his/ her answers. Think about a person getting deposed, and then is questioned by their own lawyer in the deposition. No gotcha questions. No. No.

It was embarrassing for the profession of true journalism, but then, THIS is CNN.

And, I thought, stupidly, that the original cable news network couldn't get any worse.

Enjoy.

MOVE OVER CARROT TOP; WE'VE GOT "AIMLESS" and ANDY

Over the past few months, we've witnessed, some very personally, the tragedy of the Coronavirus pandemic. Wednesday night, CNN viewers got to witness another tragedy, and it was meant to be funny.

As he has often been, New York Governor Andrew Cuomo was a guest on his little brother Chris' nightly CNN broadcast, "***Cuomo Prime Time***." The Guv Cuomo has been busy over the past few months warning New Yorkers to use caution when getting in social situations as to not spread the virus. Meanwhile, his brother Chris has been busy berating President Trump on a daily basis and chastising those that violate social distancing and "stay home" orders.

The "chastisement" is rich — no it's, hypocritical-to-the-max, seeing how "journalist" Cuomo staged a fake "must-see TV" reemergence from his self-imposed basement quarantine last month as he survived his Coronavirus infection. It was soon discovered that Cuomo had actually "reemerged" the day before, putting his wife and kids in a vehicle and traveling 30 minutes to see his multimillion-dollar property in The Hamptons, where he is building a new mansion. A few days later, both his wife and one of his kids came down with the Coronavirus, securing Cuomo the "Dipsh-t of the Week" and "Hypocrite of the Month" awards.

On Wednesday night, The Brothers Cuomo decided it was time for a comedy routine regarding the Governor's recent virus test in which a swab was stuck up his nose. Chris thought it would be "hilarious" to show the "actual swab" used to go up the Governor's ample schnoz. As FOX's Greg Gutfeld insightfully observed, it was a gag right out of a prop-comic Carrot Top routine. The swab was feet long with its top the size of a watermelon. The Governor could not contain his laughter as his little brother was "entertaining" his audience on what seemed like an "Open Mike Night" on CNN.

I thought 'ol Andy was going to fall off his chair guffawing when Chris joked that the giant swab was needed to "fit up that double-barrel shotgun that you have mounted on the front of your pretty face." Stop it, please, my sides are hurting!

The Brothers Cuomo thought their routine was comedy that Abbott and Costello would have been proud of. It wasn't. It was sad, sick, and perhaps the most inappropriate thing I have witnessed during the pandemic, especially when you consider the players: a holier-than-thou "journalist," who berates and scolds others, and the governor of the state hardest hit by the Coronavirus, who, through his crack health team, ordered infected elderly folks back into their retirement homes to die and kill others via exposure– more than 5,000 elderly souls.

Of course, Governor Cuomo couldn't bring himself to take the blame for the deadly decision concerning the elderly in his state. Oh, that's a big no-no. First, he threw his state health commissioner under the bus, and then recently decided it was the fault of "the White House and the CDC."

But, that, and Chris Cuomo's fake reemergence and infecting his own family with the virus, was all in the past. It was time to move on. And, what better way to move on than a "classic" comedy routine on national television.

Governor "Jimmy Durante" Cuomo should be ashamed of himself and apologize, not only to his fellow New Yorkers, but, to all

Americans. After all, MSNBC's Trump-hating host Joy Reid called the Governor "a kind of acting president."

As for "Typhoid Chris" Cuomo, he should be fired. Period. Maybe he can join the crew at *"Saturday Night Live,"* as they seem to be a bit low on comedy "talent."

NO VOTER FRAUD? CHECK YOUR "FACTS" FACT CHECKERS!

What happens when a Liberal "fact-checking" website that calls itself "the definitive fact-checking resource" can't get its story straight and I see clear evidence of that what the fact-checking site declares "isn't happening" is actually "happening?" I call it confusion, or fraud, while the "definitive fact-checking" site calls it "conflation."

On April 24, 2020, the RealClearPolitics website published an article by Mark Hemingway, headlined "28 Million Mail-In Ballots Went Missing in Last Four Elections." Based on a report from the Public Interest Legal Foundation (PILF), using data from the U.S. Election Assistance Commission (EAC), RealClearPolitics was putting a spotlight on the danger of moving America to a voting-by-mail system.

The "underlying" issue has become white-hot as the Coronavirus pandemic continues in this country as we approach summer. The Left believes the "only" way we can have a "fair" election this fall is if we allow voting by mail, assuming "no one," for fear of spreading the virus in NOVEMBER, will be able to get to a polling booth to cast their vote, let alone have a valid "voter suppression" photo I.D. Ahem. Oh, those folks can go to Safeway, Target, Home Depot, a lottery ticket line, a liquor store and a weed dispensary, but NOT a voting station?

Hmm.

The REAL issue that the "fact checkers" at Snopes decided to tackle is what RealClearPolitics has brought to our attention: "Between 2012 and 2018, (an estimated) 28.3 million mail-in ballots remain unaccounted for, according to data from the federal Election Assistance Commission. The missing ballots amount to nearly one in five of all absentee ballots and ballots mailed to voters residing in states that do elections exclusively by mail."

Snopes determined that claim was a "mixture" of "truth" and "lies." If you are as wary of Snopes' political viewpoint as I am, a determination of "mixture" means the story is TRUE, and they are biting their tongue admitting so. But let me allow Snopes to hang themselves with their own words. Oh, and don't forget, I have REAL evidence I will show you later thanks to a Facebook friend, and my countless hours watching every single frickin' episode of "Law and Order: Special Victims Unit" during this "stay-at-home" incarceration.

I will cut to the chase: According to Snopes, "States and local authorities simply have NO IDEA what happened to these ballots since they were mailed – and the figure of 28 million missing ballots is likely even higher because some areas in the country, notably Chicago, did not respond to the federal agency's survey questions. This figure does not include ballots that were spoiled, undeliverable, or came back for any reason."

But then Snopes went further, calling on one of their "experts" to debunk that the voter-fraud claim by author Mark Hemingway, who used the term "missing" to describe ballots that were mailed out to voters, but not officially cast by those voters.

"Election officials 'DON'T KNOW' what happened to those ballots," said Paul Gronke, a professor at Reed College, who is the director of the Early Voting Information Center. "They were received by eligible citizens and not filled out. Where are they now? Most likely, in landfills."

BUT Snopes said: "Conflating (there's that word) voters choosing not to cast their ballot with 'missing' ballots is a fundamental flaw in the argument ... The simple fact is a ballot not cast is not a missing ballot."

WAIT! Your own expert, Snopes, says "WE DON'T KNOW" what happened to these ballots, yet you folks "assume" they were "uncast." Not missing, not tossed away in a scandal of epic proportions, considering we are talking about 28 million votes and clear and present danger of voter fraud!

OK, enough faulty fact checking and hyperbole. How about some real s—t?

Last week, I got an email from a Facebook friend in Michigan. He has received FOUR absentee voting applications in his mailbox. One for him and three for supposedly previous residents of his current address. (A photo accompanies this post. I had my friend disguise the names of the other "residents" of his humble abode.)

The Michigan election leader, Democrat Secretary of State Jocelyn Benson, had sent out these "applications" for absentee voting to ALL Michigan residents. And obviously, you will see, a "few" more. President Trump, wrongly, said the Michigan election official had broken the law by "sending out absentee ballots." The mass mailing was actually "applications" to vote, and not ballots. However, doing so, whether ballots, or applications to all Michigan residents, WAS illegal.

So, could my friend commit a crime, seemingly endorsed by the Michigan Democratic political machine? Perhaps. All he has to do is fill out the "non-him" application forms, sign with a squiggly signature (think how you sign on the pay pads at the grocery store) and eventually get three absentee ballots from previous residents of his home in addition to the one assigned to his name.

Voter fraud? I guess it is, as Snopes says, a "mixture." Kind of like when I add cow manure and bone meal to my potting soil, only to have my wife say, "Geez, Jason, our garden smells like s—t!"

CHRIS CUOMO: "I'VE FALLEN AND I CAN'T GET UP!"

CNN "star" Typhoid Chris Cuomo says that since contracting the Coronavirus in late March, he is still a bit "under the weather." But, it might just be the result of a self-inflicted "high-pressure front" or "storm clouds" on the horizon. Or, maybe, just maybe, it's a bogus forecast.

Two months ago, the CNN anchor announced with great fanfare that he had been infected with the virus and "heroically" proclaimed he would self-quarantine in his basement and broadcast his ***"Cuomo Prime Time"*** show from his isolated and lonely bunker in order to spare his family from the potentially deadly scourge. His announcement, temporarily, made his audience ratings soar, besting his avowed cable TV enemy, FOX's Sean Hannity, while also topping MSNBC's Rachel Maddow.

During his "selfless" quarantine, Cuomo nightly would chastise New Yorkers, hell all Americans, who chose to ignore social distancing guidelines and wear a face mask. After all, Cuomo was personally trying to save the world, so why shouldn't everyone?

Then, on April 21, it was revealed that Cuomo was a big, fat liar. In a live, must-see TV event on April 13, Cuomo "reemerged" from his bunker, supposedly Coronavirus-free, and emotionally cheered that his life was back to normal and could rejoin his loving family for the first time in weeks. As I wrote then, it was a scene much more dramatic than when Lassie "came home" to little Timmy.

But there was a problem: Cuomo had actually "re-emerged" the day before, Easter Sunday, packed his family into his vehicle and drove 30 minutes to his property in The Hamptons, where he is building a multimillion-dollar mansion. No one would have known about Cuomo's clandestine family adventure, but 'ol Chris decided to get into a verbal confrontation on his new property with a local resident who had questioned why the TV star was out and about considering he had made such a big whoop about his isolation.

When the news broke nine days later, Cuomo was exposed as a fibber. For what purpose? Most likely audience ratings. More on that in a bit. Oh, by the way, just a few days after Hamptonsgate, Cuomo's wife and son came down with the Coronavirus. Thanks Honey. Thanks Dad.

But Cuomo wasn't done being stupid. Earlier this month, in one of his regular, nauseating on-air sessions with his older brother, New York Governor and "retirement home executioner" Andrew Cuomo, Chris tried to perform a comedy sketch about his brother's recent Coronavirus test, showing his audience the "alleged" ginormous swab used to jam up the Governor's large booger vault. Governor Cuomo had a difficult time containing his laughter as his little brother "played around." Both Cuomos were publicly slayed for making light of the Coronavirus testing situation, and the Cuomo Brothers Comedy Act had a run of just one show before getting the hook.

So where is our "hero" today? Earlier this week on his show, Chris told Dr. Sanjay Gupta that he had "weird stuff going on" with his lungs and "funky stuff" in his blood work. As an EMT in high school and in college myself, and thus a "medical expert," I quickly surmised that the "weird and funky stuff" was most likely caused by having one's head firmly planted in the southern hemisphere of the body. But what do I know? If Chris Cuomo says "stuff" is going on, then we MUST take him at his word.

Cuomo told Gupta: "I'm not back to where I was before I had the virus, but I can work." What a super trooper: obviously not "fully recovered" from the Coronavirus, but willing to take one for the team.

Then, Cuomo couldn't help himself, promoting his status of being "God's gift to everyone," saying he wants to donate blood to help with research, BUT has found out that his organs haven't returned to how they were before he contracted the virus. So, no blood from our "hero," but he did say he was currently donating PLASMA.

According to their official website, plasma donation is just swell with the U.S. FDA, which encourages Coronavirus SURVIVORS to donate plasma to help fight the disease. That is, after they have FULLY RECOVERED. If the plasma donation is true, is Typhoid Chris Cuomo risking the health of others just as he did with his family jaunt to The Hamptons?

Maybe this is all about audience ratings, because since his infection, his isolation, his phony "reemergence" and the rise and fall of the Cuomo Brothers Comedy, Cuomo's "demo" ratings (folks 25 to 54) have been in a free fall. According to Nielsen Media Research out this week, Cuomo's ratings have declined by a stunning 49 percent since April 1, 2020. His ratings drop dwarfed the declines experienced by Hannity's and Maddow. First place Hannity ratings are off 38 percent, while Maddow is down seven percent. But Hannity is smoking Cuomo with 225,000 more viewers nightly, and Maddow has topped him for the first time in a long while.

A spokesperson for Chris Cuomo declined to comment on his ratings disaster.

My suggestion is that Cuomo go back into self-isolation and throw a "pity party" for himself. At least he can surround himself with people who believe his tales of trials and tribulations and "comedy magic."

CHAPTER SEVEN

JOSEPH BIDEN AND THE TECHNICOLOR FINGER PUPPET

BIDEN CALLS MICHIGAN GUV WHITMER: IT WASN'T PRETTY

SATIRE

My totally unreliable sources tell me they have audio tape of a call, two hours ago, between Democratic Presidential nominee Joe Biden and Michigan Governor Gretchen Whitmer. I have not checked the veracity of this audio tape, but it came to me on a CASSETTE, so I know it is real.

WHITMER: Hello, Mr. Vice President, how are you doing?

BIDEN: Doing, doing what? I just woke up. Who is this?

WHITMER: Michigan Governor Gretchen Whitmer. You know, you are grooming me to be your VP?

BIDEN: I never touched you, sweetheart, um, remembering, re-membering, I recall smelling your hair –it smelled fantastic. Is that Clairol or Suave?

WHITMER: Sir, please DO NOT mention RECALL, OK? Ah, we have a situation here in Lansing.

BIDEN: Yeah, I know, my son Hunter put big money on Michigan State winning the Final Four and then this silly virus screwed up everything. My son lost a boatload in pre-bets, but then, he has plenty. I mean, Christ on a Crutch, plenty.

WHITMER: No sir, here's the deal: I have thousands of Michiganders driving around my office on the streets of the Michigan state capitol calling for my head.

BIDEN: My, my, no man should demand "head." That is so wrong, without a great, expensive dinner and after-dinner drinks. Oh, and flowers.

WHITMER: No sir, I think you misunderstand: They are calling for my "head on a platter."

BIDEN: Boy, that is a new one to me. I think I might call my great friend Bill Clinton to get some advice on this kerfuffle. He is so, so good at that. Nice plates? Fine China?

WHITMER: Jesus Joe, I have people with pitchforks and KKK hoods surrounding the capitol building.

BIDEN: KKK hoods? Really?

WHITMER: Well, kinda hoods – red baseball hats with the evil "Keep America Great" emblazoned on the front, obviously sent from the fire of Satan, with pitchforks.

BIDEN: Well, wow, first, Satan is on our Election Board, so I doubt that, but, obviously, those wackos DID NOT get those pitchforks at Home Depot or Lowes seeing how you closed off the gardening centers at those stores. Hmmm, I am in a quandary.

WHITMER: Mr. Biden, are you willing to help me in my time of need?

BIDEN: Well, chickee, um, er, Governor Whitsomething, ah, Greta, I have a lot on my plate. Just today I got an endorsement from Barack Obama and Liz Warren, although the latter is like a one-dollar lottery winning ticket – you throw it in the side pocket of your driver's door of your car and it gets sucked out at the car wash. You say, "whatever, a buck."

WHITMER: Mr. Vice President, I AM DESPERATE!!

BIDEN: I know you are, Genna, and I am here to help you even though I have no idea where the hell I am.

BIDEN GETS MAJOR ENDORSEMENT HE CAN'T FATHOM
SATIRE

It's been a banner day for presumed Democratic Presidential candidate Joe Biden. While quarantined in his mansion in Delaware, tragically failing to put a Sesame Street puzzle together – "Good Lord, there has to be 20 pieces here! Where do I start?" – and listening to his wife, Dr. Jill, repeating to him, "You don't remember Tara Reade, you don't remember Tara Reade, you don't remember Tara Reade, now take a nappy-nappy little Joey," Biden scored a coup.

"Honey," Jill Biden said, awakening Joe from his perch in his backyard hammock. "You got a major endorsement today from one of the biggest organizations in the world."

"Are we in the Bahamas, honey?" Biden said, still sleepy-eyed.

"No, honey, we are in our backyard here in Delaware," she cooed.

"I had the most awful dream, Jill. I was on a beach in the Bahamas, and this young former staffer, very, very hot by the way, came up to me, holding a baby. The poor little kid had hair plugs, for crissake! Then I woke up."

"I told you to wipe that out of your memory, honey."

"My what?"

"Your memory, dear."

"Oh, yeah, I forgot."

"Anyway, Joe, Mister Former eight-year Vice President of The United States, and soon to be, ta-da, El Jefe Grande, I have great news."

"We're moving to Mexico?"

"No, dumbass, you received a huge endorsement today from the UAW."

"The UAW, really? Oh, I love those women. I have been supportive of the United Arab Women as long as I know. They are smart, intelligent and smart. Although, to be frank, their hair smells a bit like hummus. But, no one is perfect. Boy can those gals grow facial hair. No wonder they wear those Hijibabbatollays."

"Joe, they are called Hijabs, you dork. Anyway, the UAW is NOT the United Arab Women: it is the United Auto Workers."

"Oh, those guys. Barack and I bailed them out back in 1945. They owe me."

"Honey, you probably already know, but the United Auto Workers have a big issue with corruption these days. A lot of their top executives are in prison or are going to prison, and you may have to deal with that as President."

"Pardon me?"

"Yes, Joe, you will probably need to issue a boatload of pardons for these UAW folks your first week in office."

"This is my first week in office? Boy, time sure flies, Joan."

JOE BIDEN: HIS FINGER ON THE PULSE OF, UM, ER, NEVERMIND

SATIRE

Well, well, it is now apparent the "Tara Reade" story about an unwanted sexual encounter with Democratic President candidate Joe Biden won't go away, now that video has been unearthed, allegedly showing a call-in from Reade's mother to Larry King Live back in the early 90s, weeks after the alleged encounter.

The "*Larry King Live*" show aired on CNN at the time, so it is obvious that CNN unearthed this video. Ah, no. The Media Research Council did. Yes, a conservative group, but regardless, the video is real and stunning and, unlike the Ballsy Ford allegations against Judge Kavanaugh, seems to back the claims of sexual impropriety, hell, rape, against Uncle Joe.

I wonder what a Joe Biden interview on this subject NOW would look like in the wake of his staffers claiming all charges are false. Hmmm?

FOX News' Martha McCallum (MM): Mr. former Vice President, thank you for joining me tonight.

BIDEN: Honey, I never touched you.

MM: No sir, and I am not suggesting you did. Tell me, are the charges against you by your former staffer Tara Reade, false, as your staff has indicated previously?

BIDEN: I can't remember.

MM: Well, can you remember what you had for breakfast this morning?

BIDEN: Break Fast? Yes, I need to break fast from this horrible story.

MM: No sir, what did you eat this morning?

BIDEN: I don't remember but there are a whole lot of folks trying to eat my lunch, if you know what I mean, Rachel.

MM: It's Martha, and this is FOX, not MSNBC.

BIDEN: Yes, Greta, you certainly are a fox. I can almost smell your hair through this computer-thinga-ma-jiggy I am staring into. I think it's called Snipe. Wow, think about it: last week the TV was invented and today, I can talk with you on a lap dance.

MM: Sir, it is called a "laptop."

BIDEN: Well, of course you can be on top. You just say when and where.

MM: Mr. Biden, let me cut to the chase.

BIDEN: Chase? Hell no, those bastards are crooks. I prefer the Hong Kong and Shanghai Bank of China, HSBC. They get all my business, savings, checking debits, and, I set up an education account for my son, little Hunter.

MM: Sir, Hunter is a grown man in his 40s.

BIDEN: Boy, they grow up so fast. One minute I am changing his diapers and the next day he is sipping champagne on an Air Force Two flight to China. Is this country great or what?

HILLARY GETS BEHIND JOE BIDEN: THANK GOD! SHE IS SAFE THERE!

SATIRE ALERT: Before reading this entry, please put down the Lysol or Clorox-and-tonic double shot. Put down the BB gun, it cannot kill you in a million years. Just read and relax.

So, Hillary Clinton came "out" today and, via video stream, endorsed Joe Biden for President. For her, Hillary, it must have been like pulling crooked teeth out of an Arkansas hooker her husband's security forces had left by the side of a rural Little Rock gravel road. "Sand her fingerprints! Sand her fingerprints, dammit!" "Madam First Lady, she has no hands." "Oh, hell fellas, WHAT DIFFERENCE, AT THIS POINT, DOES IT MAKE!"

While endorsing Biden's crippled crawl to the Democratic National Convention in Swillwaukee this summer, Clinton spoke optimistically about Biden's chances of victory over the evil incumbent Donald J. Trump. As Hillary spoke, perky as the sloth on those funny Progressive insurance ads, she thankfully could not see 'ol Joe Biden napping on screen.

No, Jason, he was just being solemn, like Nancy "Ben and Jerry's" Pelosi, and "prayerful," cherishing the moment of an endorsement from an old rival and a powerful, um, er, political, um, ah, force.

No, he was napping. Period. If you play back the video and zoom in, there was drool coming out of Biden's mouth. AM I THE ONLY ONE THAT WATCHES LAW AND ORDER SPECIAL VICTIMS' UNIT??!!!???

Anyway, Hillary is ALL IN for Uncle Joe, the Finger Puppet Master. She, of all people, knows the havoc created by men acting badly. Hell, based on her "past," she may be like the famous forger played by Leonardo DiCaprio in the movie Catch Me If You Can, who turned out to be a great buster of criminals today.

From now on, I think Hillary Clinton will not add the hashtag #MeToo to her posts. It might be #Iamjusttryingtoberelevent or #HaveyouseenmyworthlesshusbandithinkthatPOSisinthecaymansgettinglaidagain.

OBAMA TO BIDEN: I'M GONNA KEEP ON LOVING YOU!

SATIRE: *Warning? Please do not drink a shot of Lysol or Clorox before reading this. Items in the mirror are closer than they actually appear. Reading this satiric post may cause, nausea, vomiting,* *high blood pressure and anal leakage. Call the offices of Mi, Butz and Hertz at 800-Mibutzhertz or 800-642-8894.*

Former two-term President Barack Hussein Obama has reportedly reached out to his VP, Joe Biden, to give him advice on the current Presidential campaign and offer solace for Biden's increasingly exposed sexual assault travails. Below is believed to be, according to my totally unreliable sources, the content of that phone call, yesterday, from Mr. Obama's $8 million D.C. mansion and Biden's "quarantined" bunker in his basement in Delaware.

BIDEN: Hello, it's former Vice President and current Democratic Presidential nominee Joe Biden. Is this "that woman from Michigan." Gretchen Whitmer?

BHO: No, Joe, you dumbass, it's Barack!

BIDEN: Brach! I didn't order any candy. Oh well, Halloween is just days away. Glad you called.

BHO: Jesus, Joe, it's your old boss, Barack Obama!

BIDEN: Obama? Obama? Obama? Oh, that reggae group. I love their music. Is this K-Tel Records?

BHO: Joe, IT'S PRESIDENT Barack Obama.

BIDEN: Oh…Hey man! Long time no talk.

BHO: Joe, I need to speak "frankly" about these alleged sexual assault charges which seem to be exploding right now.

BIDEN: Well, Frank, go ahead. Like Ross Perot, I am all ears.

BHO: FOX News is "hunting" you down right now, my friend.

BIDEN: No, no, Michelle, my son Hunter is fine and has a lovely daughter, my new grandchild.

BHO: But Joe, the polls are going to go the wrong way.

BIDEN: You're right, I keep telling my new little grandchild to "watch Mommy on the pole, watch Mommy on the pole. You'll get it."

BHO: Joe, get serious. We have a dastardly President in Trump that has multiple sexual assault allegations against him and, on camera, said he likes to grab, um, er, the P-word, yet YOU are the one in the news regarding bad sexual behavior.

BIDEN: You are so right, Osama. Grabbing is wrong when you can let your fingers do the walking.

BHO: Joe! This could bring you down.

BIDEN: Is this the "white person" down, where "down" is bad, or the "Black dude" down, where "down" is actually good?

BHO: It's BAD, Joe!

BIDEN: Is it the "bad," as in what Charles Manson did, or the "bad" in the Michael Jackson chart-topping song?

BHO: Joe, are you binging on old MTV videos?

BIDEN: Hey, Barack, even as I wander, I'm keeping you in sight. You're a candle in the window on the cold, dark winter's night. And I'm getting closer than I ever thought, I, I, might.

BHO: (Click.)

#BELIEVEWOMEN #BELIEVEJOEBIDEN
#BELIEVEWHATEVER #RIPLEYSBELIEVEORDONT

Is there a difference between the sexual harassment charges against then-Supreme Court nominee Brent Kavanaugh and former VP Joe Biden? Kavanaugh was "guilty until proven innocent" according to the Left, including Hawaii Congress woman Hirono, who told male detractors who were pro-Kavanaugh to "Shut Up and Step Up!" She led a #Believewomenyoustupidmen! #BelieveWomenmovement.

Several Democratic Senators, even before the Kavanaugh hearings were completed in their chamber, went on camera and proclaimed they "believed" Kavanaugh's accuser, Christine B. Ford. Of course, Ms. Ford listed a few corroborators to her "claim," yet they, her close friends back in the '80s during the alleged transgression, ALL punted. No memory, whatsoever, of the claim. Ahem.

Apparently, there was nothing "there there." But the Left still believed Kavanaugh was guilty…of something nefarious. So much so, CongressNut Maxine Waters promised to IMPEACH Kavanaugh once sitting on his bench in the Supreme Court.

#Kavanaughesguiltyofsomething! #Impeachkavanaugh!

Fast-forward to today: Joe Biden's female sexual assault accuser is "not to be believed."

#JOEISNOTGUILTY #TARAREADEISAWHORE #BIDEN-HADARTHRITISFORYEARSANDHASNOCONTROLOFHIS FINGERS

The MSM is working overtime to find a "crack" in Tara Reade's accusation. The latest? NBC News reports that Reade says she's "not sure" what wording she used in "the complaint she alleges to have filed with a Senate personnel office concerning Joe Biden." She has said, according to NBC News, that the complaint, if it's found, would not include the "literal" sexual assault accusation.

To be fair, former Biden staffer Tara Reade told NBC News that she is "not sure" about the language used in her alleged sexual assault Senate complaint. It was back in 1993. That was 27 years ago. Hell, I cannot remember yesterday's breakfast, let alone the words I used in a nasty company memo 27 years ago. Remember the EXACT words you said to your kid or a friend back in 1993? Oh, I do remember a couple of words to my little boys: "Lift the frickin' toilet seat when you pee!" (Sorry, I am lying. My wife said that.)

But Jason, wouldn't you remember what you wrote or said concerning a major issue in your life? Yeah, maybe. I remember "I do" and "You're pregnant? Um, er, great, honey!" Other than that, I cannot testify to any words I said or wrote almost three decades ago. And, I certainly could not remember off the top of my head the EXACT words that I would have written in a sexual harassment complaint 27 years ago.

But for NBC News, it is a "gotcha" moment in a pure biased effort to bolster Biden against the much-hated President Trump. And, it is the first supposed CRACK in the case the media is PROSECUTING now against Tara Reade to defend the Finger Puppet Joe Biden.

#BELIEVEWOMENBUTJOEBIDENISINNOCENT #METOOTHINKBIDENISGUILTYBUTLETSQUIETLYCLOSEOUREYESFORTHEGREATERGOOD #VOTEBIDENLETHIMDIEINOFFICEANDHILLARYISPRESIDENT #PERFECTPLAN

My message to Tara Reade: Listen to Hawaii Congresswoman Hirono and do the opposite: Don't Shut Up! Stay strong.

JOE, HUNTER AND AN ATM

SATIRE: *Do not inject Lysol, Clorox or Pool Supplies while reading this.*

HUNTER: Dad, hi. I wanted to call you to wish you an early Father's Day. I sent you flowers from Amazon Prime and they should arrive tomorrow. Jeff Bezos personally picked them out. He loves you.

JOE: Son, this Sunday is MOTHER'S Day. I know as I told my scheduler to book me on TV shows on Memorial Day this weekend, to honor the troops, and she corrected me. Damn, July is a busy month in this country.

HUNTER: Oh, yeah, right, dude, I mean Dad. Hey, what is the PIN number on the Visa card you gave me?

JOE: You need a Visa? When did you become Chinese? I knew your Mom was a free spirit just before I met her, but I didn't know you were Chinese.

HUNTER: Dad, dammit, I took your Visa credit card out of your wallet the last time I saw you in your basement quarantine in Delaware.

JOE: Jesus son, I TOLD you I wanted to give you CREDIT for your accomplishments in life after being a crack addict. Shit, you stole my Visa card?

HUNTER: I borrowed it Dad. (Sniff, snort) Now, I need the frickin' PIN number, OK?

JOE: Try "TRUMP SUCKS."

HUNTER: Dad, it has to be a four-digit number for crissake!

JOE: Hey, Hey, Pal, no reason to take our former President's name in vain!

HUNTER: Dad, I got guys here with "merchandise" that need their payment. I need the damned PIN number, now!

JOE: Oh hell, try 007; you know I used to be on the Senate Intelligence Committee.

HUNTER: DAD! It has to a four-digit number. Hurry. These guys are getting pissed!

JOE: H-I-L-L, um, B-I-L-L, oh damn, those aren't it. Oh wait! It's "Maxine WATERS!" That's four digits, W-A-T-E-R-S!"

CLICK.

BIDEN AND OBAMA: THE UNMASKED SINGERS
SATIRE

My totally unreliable sources have done it again, this time getting the audio of a call yesterday between former President Barack Obama and his former VP, Democratic Presidential candidate Joe Biden. Although I cannot vouch for the authenticity of this recording, as usual, I will abide by today's standard MSM protocol and share it with the world anyway. If it turns out to be fake, I will graciously kind-of apologize, blaming it on others.

BIDEN: Hello, this is Joe, who is this?

BHO: It's 44.

BIDEN: 44? 44? Oh! Is this the Delaware Lottery? Did I win the Lucky Pick 3?

BHO: Jesus!

BIDEN: Jesus? Am I dead? Is this heaven? Damn! Oops, I meant Darn! But it looks a lot like Delaware.

BHO: Joe, it's Hussein.

BIDEN: See! I told all those Republican rednecks not to be mean to the Muslims cuz there was a 50/50 chance Jesus was one of "those" people.

BHO: For God's sake Joe, it's your former boss, the President of the United States, Barack Hussein Obama.

BIDEN: Oh, hey man!

BHO: Joe, you can't use my name anymore on this call. The Trump team is probably wiretapping your phone.

BIDEN: Are you telling me Trump hired Comey, Brennan and Clapper to do his dirty work? Those turncoat bastards!

BHO: No Joe, it's that we can't be too sure anymore. Anyway, we've got some big trouble and by "We," I mean, "You."

BIDEN: What have I done? I've been stuck in my basement for months now.

BHO: It's all about the "Unmasking" scandal.

BIDEN: Well, it IS a scandal. I mean, it's my favorite TV show, but that little Chinaman judge, while hilarious, can't seem to get anything right.

BHO: Joe, not the TV show "The Masked Singer," you dumbass.

And, please, don't call the Asian American judge Ken Jeong a "Chinaman." He's Vietnamese.

BIDEN: Ah well Barack, as they say, tomato, potato, ah, er, you know the rest, man.

BHO: Stop it, Joe! And quit using my name on this call. Anyway, I'm talking about members of my team, including you, unmasking Lt. General Mike Flynn to get him fired and eventually nail Trump.

BIDEN: I don't know anything about that, whomever I am talking to that could be the former President.

BHO: Joe, the gig is up. The DOJ, two mouth-breathing Republican Senators and now the media have the files showing you participated in the investigation of Mike Flynn.

BIDEN: Oh, yes, George, I did know about that, um, about the investigation, ah, ah, er, um, just not the prosecution of Glenn.

BHO: It's Flynn not Glenn, numbnuts! And I am not Good Morning America's George Stephanopoulos.

BIDEN: Then, doggone it, who am I talking with?

BHO: Your old boss for crying out loud!

BIDEN: Mr. Phillips, the pharmacist from the Rexall drug store in Scranton when I was a teenager? I thought you were dead.

BHO: Your last boss, Joe.

BIDEN: Is this my buddy Barack?

BHO: I told you NOT to use my name!

BIDEN: Sorry. What do you want me to do?

BHO: A ton of my Administration is fingered in this probe –

BIDEN: Hey wait just a gall-darn-minute, that's a bunch of malarkey. I did not touch that woman!

BHO: No Joe, please focus. A bunch of my team unmasked Mike Flynn in the days leading up to Trump taking office back in 2017, including you. Now while there was nothing illegal about that, one of my team members leaked the information to *The Washington Post* and that ARE illegal, a 10-year felony.

BIDEN: You know, Bar-, um, I mean, whomever this is, it is starting to come back to me. Yeah, I remember a meeting in that building, the, the, er, um –

BHO: The White House?

BIDEN: Yeah, I think that's what it's called, and I remember you specifically telling the team to get this into the media.

BHO: Joe, are you telling me you can remember THAT, but you can't remember what you had for breakfast this morning?

BIDEN: What's breakfast?

BHO: Oh lord. Joe, here's what I need you to do. The next time you do an interview or, God help us, appear before a Congressional committee, I need you to emphatically say that I was not a part of this unmasking of General Flynn.

BIDEN: Gotcha! If they ask me, I will say, "I was not a part of this unmasking of General Flynn." Anything else?

BHO: No, Joe! You need to say that I, President Obama, "was not a part of the unmasking of General Flynn."

BIDEN: Barack? Is that you?

BHO: CLICK

BIDEN AND WARREN "POW WOW" FOR CAMPAIGN VIDEO
SATIRE

———

News item from "The Hill": "Former Vice President Joe Biden and Sen. Elizabeth Warren (D-Mass.) teamed up to call several small-dollar donors to his presidential campaign for a new video released Sunday by the Biden campaign.

"In the video, Biden and Warren thank several of the former vice president's supporters for their donations, mirroring videos released by Warren during her own campaign for the Democratic nomination over the past year.

"Warren became known during her own presidential bid for personally calling supporters and thanking them for their generosity. The Massachusetts senator is reportedly on a shortlist of potential vice-presidential picks for Biden, who is now the Democratic Party's presumptive nominee and has pledged to select a woman to run on the ticket with him."

That's the news, but here's the skinny. This video came into being after a conference call between Biden, Warren and DNC Chairman Tom "FU" Perez. My totally unreliable sources gave me a bootleg copy of that phone call and I am pleased to share it with the world.

PEREZ: Welcome to both of you. This is an exciting time for our party. The Coronavirus is still crushing the Orangeman and we, thank God, see no end in sight, especially with the continued help of our "Lockdown A-Team" -- NYC Mayor deBlasio, Michigan Governor Gretchen Whitmer and Los Angeles Mayor Garcetti -- making certain that the SAFETY of the November Election, um, I mean our voters, ah, er, I mean our citizens, is paramount.

BIDEN: Paramount? I remember when that Hollywood studio was created back in 1912. I was a young'un then, but boy was it exciting, seeing those first silent movies. I was speechless.

PEREZ: Joe, ah, never mind. I want to thank you, Senator Warren, for agreeing to do this video with Joe. It will show both the unity of our party and our concerns for the "little people."

BIDEN: We're putting midgets in our video?

WARREN: Jesus Joe, you don't call them "midgets!"

BIDEN: Who is that?

PEREZ: Joe, it's Liz Warren. You know, a former rival that endorsed you last month.

BIDEN: Warren? Warren? Warren? Oh, you mean Pocahontas!

PEREZ: Joe, that is the awful nickname Rush Limbaugh gave her. Stop it! It is beneath you.

BIDEN: I never did anything with her! Isn't that right, Lori? Besides, my staff tells me I am considering you as potential running mate, although I am not sure for what.

WARREN: First of all, Joe, my name is Elizabeth or Liz. Secondly, I prefer to be referred to as "Chief Running Mate." It honors my Native American roots.

BIDEN: I thought that was a bunch of malarkey, Lisa? Really, what kind of "Indian" are you? Are you the peace-pipe-smoking brand or the "Welcome to 7/11" brand? I gotta know so I don't step in something.

PEREZ: OK Joe, enough of this crap. We need to get down to brass tacks.

BIDEN: Yes, by all means, let's talk about raising TAXES. When can we start? I mean, now that we are in the White House, we can't burn any sunlight, or as Geronimo once told me, "Let's get it on."

PEREZ: Brass TACKS, Joe, Brass Tacks. We want to steal a great idea from Elizabeth's campaign and make it work for you.

BIDEN: This isn't plagiarizing, is it? I learned my lesson on that sucker.

PEREZ: No, Joe, Senator Warren will call average, everyday donors and thank them for their support. We want to have you do the same for your presidential campaign, film it and use it as a campaign video proving that you are not beholden to big corporate money, and care deeply about the little people.

BIDEN: There you go again with tossing mid-, I mean, dwarfs, into the mix. For the life of me, I haven't been able to tell the difference between the two since Dorothy landed in Oz. I mean, stuck here in my basement, I have been binge-watching reruns of "Little People, Big World" on TLC cable and, to be honest, it just gives me the "willies." But, boy, is it addictive.

WARREN: Mr. Vice President, with all due respect, for which I have none, please, please, SHUT UP!

PEREZ: I see this is really going to work. OK, here is what we do. Liz calls a few donors and thanks them for their financial support, whether it be five bucks or a hundred, and we juxtapose that on a split-screen video with you, Joe, doing the same thing.

BIDEN: Wait a minute! If I do the same thing and call the same people, isn't that a waste of time and money?

PEREZ: No, Joe, you call other people.

BIDEN: Are they "little people?" I mean, they probably have little, tiny wallets.

PEREZ: Wait a second Joe, I need to take a hit off of, um, er, ah, I mean I need a few Advils. (Sound of inhalation.) Ahh, there.

BIDEN: Advil? Tom, do you have a fever?

PEREZ: I am getting one.

BIDEN: Great! Then that's TWO more Coronavirus infections to add to the leader board.

PEREZ: Two?

BIDEN: Yep, one for "Tom P." and one for "T. Perez."

PEREZ: Joe, I like your savvy, but that is lying.

BIDEN: Tom, I prefer to call it "speaking with a forked tongue," right Chief Running Mate?

JOE BIDEN: IN "GOD'S NAME"

OK, Joe Biden, it is apparent you cannot think on your own, so you rely on staff to give you stuff to say. I get it. The presumptive Democratic presidential nominee (Presumptive is a Latin word that means, "oh cripes, is that all we got?" Trust me.) scorned President Trump today for taking hydroxychloroquine, plus zinc, in an effort to prevent contracting the Coronavirus.

"It's like saying, 'Maybe if you inject Clorox into your blood, it may cure you,' Biden "read" at a Yahoo News town hall on COVID-19 and food insecurity. "C'mon, man! What is he doing? What in God's name is he doing?"

I don't know, Joe, what in God's name is he doing?

Biden was not done. "There's no serious medical person out there saying to use that drug," Biden said. "It's counterproductive. It's not going to help, but the president, he decided that's an answer."

No, 'ol Joe, he decided it was the answer for him. By the way, compadre, there are LOTS of medical "persons" out there that say Hydro Chloroquine works. Just ask the Democrat State Representative from Detroit that says it saved her life.

"Look at the studies that have been done. It does much more harm than good. This is totally irresponsible," Biden claimed. No Joe, no studies, just opinions. You cannot do a "quality" study in two or three months.

Ah, Joe, the drug is FDA-approved and has been used with great success for 70 years to combat malaria and Lupus. It is NOT Clorox. It is NOT Lysol. Nice try to conflagrate two unrelated Trump incidences. I am certain a junior staffer, bathed in Clearasil, is at the bar with colleagues high-fiving the fact that you used her/ his line.

The bigger question you raise, Joe: What in God's name is he doing?

Well, I am not sure, as my discussions with God are one-way, but I hope He is listening. But I have an idea of what President Trump is doing "in God's name." Making sure the supply of face masks is growing thanks to working with various industries to fill the pipeline. Making test equipment at warp-speed to determine how wide-spread the virus is and whether or not the "curve" is flattening out. Putting an A-team together to quickly find a vaccine despite the fact we still don't have real vaccines for plagues that have harmed mankind for centuries. God be with those working on all of this.

Meanwhile, Joe, what are you doing in "God's name?" Supporting Planned Parenthood as they kill more than 350,000 healthy and harmless unborn babies EVERY year?

I don't think Lysol or Clorox will DISINFECT that, Joe!

CHAPTER EIGHT

MY LITTLE CHINA GIRL

FOR IMMMEDIATE RELEASE

NO TICKEE, NO VIRUS

SATIRE

Beijing, China APRIL 20, 2020 -- Officials from the now infamous Wahun Lab in China, long suspected source of the deadly worldwide Coronavirus, have officially come out, declaring that the lab and its scientists were not responsible for letting the virus slip out of their lab and spread across the world, killing hundreds of thousands of people so far in more than 180 countries, and Iran.

"Donard Tlump did it! He is to brame, mothelfuckels!" said Chiang Kai "Baghdad Bob" Shekky, chief spokesperson for the Chinese Communist Government Industry of Blindness and Deceit, during an emotional press conference in Beijing, attended by Chinese President Xi Jinping in a custom-made full-body condom.

"You Amelican asshores eat too much bad Chinese food flom that clappy prace, Panda Expless," he said. "Not good Chinese cuisine. Compretry lots youl stomach and obviousry youl tiny blains. You make up clap and brame us. We are innocent. Like O.J. Simpson, Lobelt Brake, you know, Baletta, and Hirraly Crinton."

At that point in the press conference, kai-Shekky, collapsed and was taken away. He complained of a high fever in the ambulance on the way to the closest trauma center in Beijing within the Soo Rong Hospital Center, but was pronounced dead, and was later cremated despite still breathing and with otherwise healthy vital signs.

KIM JONG, UH, JUNG, UH, UN, WTF, IS DEAD! MAYBE
SATIRE

DATELINE Pyongyang, North Korea: Ever the beacon of truth and transparency, North Korean "media" reports that it "seems" that the Dicktator of North Korea, Kim Jong Un, has died. The official coroner's report on Un's passing listed it as "death by Colonavilus."

In related news, NYC Mayor Bill "Big Bird" deBlasio added Kim Jong Un to his Coronavirus death count, along with a vagrant run over by a NY taxi at 2 a.m. this morning.

"That's BS!" said Un's little sister, Kim So Young.

(CORRECTION: DAMN THAT AUTOCORRECT!!!! THAT IS NOT HER NAME! I HATE YOU MARK ZUCKERBERG!)

Ah, continuing, said Un's little sister, KIM YO JONG, rumored to be eyeing the top seat now, allegedly vacated by her fat, um, er, big brother: "He didn't die of COVID-19 or what Joe Biden calls it, COVID-9," in breathtaking English that would make Geoffrey Rush blush. "Be real, motherf—ckers, he smoked five packs of Camels, Marlboros and Virginia Slims – another issue, sha! – a day. He had several dinners and some "dessert" with basketball freak and former stinky-Madonna hubby, Dennis Rodman. What you think, dumbasses? Word!"

After issuing her statement, Yo Jong said she was going back on the set of the new DIE HARD movie, starring Bruce Willis as Bruce Willis, and Yo Jong, the former Asian terrorist who supposedly died in LIVE FREE OR DIE HARD in a fiery elevator crash in an SUV, now his lover.

COMMIE TOIRET PAPEL FINARRY ALLIVES – MEGA PACK!

Stupidly, on March 17th, as the Coronavirus crisis got white-hot, I was played.

Actually, I was "prayed." Going on Google to read the latest news, a pop-up ad appeared. Thanks Mark Zuckerdouche.

The ad offered a "Mega-Pack" of toilet paper. My sphincter quivered with excitement. A mega-pack of 10 precious rolls of comfort and joy for only $34 when you couldn't find TP in the continental United States. I jumped, somewhat depressed that it would not be delivered for 10-14 days as it was coming from CHINA. Ah well, they started this mess; they might as well have a "hand" in cleaning it up.

Desperate, but still in the rapture of anticipation that would have made Mr. Whipple blush, I threw out the orange juice and any foods that had "high fiber" as I searched our house for a giant cork and duct tape.

I looked down at my bunghole and screamed, "Take a chill for a few days, you asshole!" I cried as I hugged the porcelain god, noticing that those toilet caps holding the crapper to the floor are really, really gross. "Honey, you missed a spot!" I bellowed. Not surprising, her response was for me to join Satan. After 34 years of marriage? How ungrateful and cruel.

A day after my order was made, I received CONFIRMATION that my order was SHIPPED. I looked at down at my poop chute and said," it's on the way, butthead."

And then the wait began as my weight piled up. After three weeks, I was at my s—t's end. I went back on the Chinese website to track my bounty, but to no avail. The site was no longer available. The company, and my rescue package, had evaporated. I had been had.

I immediately called the folks at Citibank and disputed the charge on my credit card. Being a good customer (meaning I charge way too much stuff), they credited my account on the spot. Got you, you Chinese Commie bastards! As they say, "He who raughs rast, raughs best!"

In the days and weeks that followed, I dutifully arose each morning at the crack of, er, ah, dawn, and stood in line at the grocery store, waiting for them to open and praying the Charmin Express supply truck had arrived that day so that I could snatch ONE package of TP – Northern, Scott's, the off-brand, whatever. Something, anything!

Then, just yesterday, I found a package in our mailbox. Forty-nine days after I had paid good money for bad toilet paper, my promised-yet-forgotten TP made its way from the Chinese mainland. The mega-pack of 10 rolls was now mine…and FREE! Chinese toilet paper apparently does not come with a "tube" in the middle of the roll. Is that the way it is in China, or are these Commie bastards just continuing to screw the world? "Good ruck, you evir Amelicans! Enjoy the wipe as we wipe you out, you stupid mothelf—kels!"

So how do I turn this chicken s—t into chicken salad? Well, personal message me your address and I will send you a roll of this Commie TP IF you PROMISE to donate $25 (or more) to your local food bank. Only 10 rolls, so act "quickry."

CHAPTER NINE

"THE FINALE"

A CRISES COLLISION AND A SICK "FEAR" IT WILL GO AWAY

The two biggest and most tragic stories of 2020 have collided in Minneapolis, where the Coronavirus pandemic and the protests-turned-violent riots in "honor" of murder victim George Floyd have hypocritically joined forces. And, sadly, some folks bent on politicizing both, are seemingly more than happy this confluence has occurred.

Yesterday, Minneapolis Democratic Mayor Jacob Frey, while declaring that the unchecked riots destroying parts of his city were largely the work of "White Supremacists" (Frey obviously got the day's "Liberal Talking Points Memo" as that notion spread throughout social media yesterday like a wild fire), decided he didn't want the "protesters" to spread the Coronavirus and began handing out hundreds of free face masks and encouraged appropriate "social distancing." Funny, from the videos, it seems that the face mask issue had already been "handled" by the "protesters"; the "social distancing," not so much.

"Hey, fellow anarchist, um, er, I mean protester, do you mind holding my Molotov cocktail while I put on this free face mask?"

"Ah, sorry dude, no can do. My hands are full of these bricks. And, hey, back off six feet, dumbass!"

Frey, along with other top Minneapolis politicians and police leaders have officially ceded parts of the city for the rioters to burn and loot as long as they "try" not to spread the Coronavirus.

At the same time, Mayor Frey is standing firm on his directive to keep churches and other houses of worship closed or strictly restricted to the pent-up faithful. Frey has gone on the record, repeatedly, warning that allowing a "suggested" 25 percent capacity in churches, et al, would be a "recipe in Minneapolis for a public disaster."

Meanwhile, thousands march, burn and loot in the streets of Minneapolis and other cities, side-by-side. I guess their "religion" is more "righteous."

The pandemic meets the "protesters" and, as I said earlier, there are some that believe this is "good" for their side, politically, because in the infamous words of Democratic politico Rahm Emmanuel, you must "never let a crisis go to waste." Wasting this dynamic duo of crises could be "deadly" for the Democrats chances in the upcoming November election.

That's not me talking: it comes from the mouths of Democratic political operatives.

Jason Furman, a former top economist in the Obama administration and now a professor at Harvard (of course), in an interview with **Politico** says that "we are about to see the best economic data we've seen in the history of this country."

Furman's point: As the Coronavirus hopefully ebbs, the economy could start rocking and rolling and that is very bad news for the Democrats hope of defeating President Trump in November. And, evidence is growing that that might just be the case.

According to **The Wall Street Journal**, "Truck loads are growing again. Air travel and hotel bookings are up slightly. Mortgage applications are rising. And more people are applying to open new businesses. For the first time since the pandemic forced widespread U.S. business closures in March, it appears conditions in some corners of the economy aren't getting worse and might even be improving."

Furman, again a Democrat, believes that "the months preceding the November election could offer Trump the chance to brag — truthfully — about the most explosive monthly employment numbers and GDP growth ever."

According to **Politico**, Furman's prediction has some Democratic strategists advising the Joe Biden campaign, apoplectic. **Politico** writes, "This is my big worry," said a former Obama White House official. Asked about the level of concern among top party officials, he said, "It's high — high, high, high, high."

If this Democratic Armageddon – a rapid economic rebound -- comes to fruition, what does Mr. Biden have to run on?

Of course, they will claim the Orangeman's response to the pandemic was slow despite the fact that the China Communist Government and the World Health Organization hid it from the world for at least two months. The Democrats will try and bury, to no avail, Joe Biden calling Trump "xenophobic" for banning travel from China to the U.S. in late January, just days after Dr. Fauci told everyone to remain calm and not panic. Democrats may also claim that Trump reopened the country too fast, and pray that the virus rears its ugly head to prove them right. Sound sick? It is.

And, of course, they will crucify Trump for "stoking" the fires of racial discrimination and violence thanks to the tragic George Floyd killing. Hell, some MSM "journalists" may even try to unearth "facts" that Trump personally directed "White Supremacists" to turn "peaceful protests" in a host of Democrat-controlled cities into all-out riots. After all, Trump and ALL of his supporters are "certified" racists, homophobes, Islamophobes, misogynists, bigots and mouth-breathing, gun-toting morons.

A DEN OF LIBERAL PHOTO THIEVES

Just days ago, June 1, when Washington D.C. was under siege thanks to looters, arsonists and other thugs among the "peaceful protestors," David A. Graham, a staffer writer at the Trump-hating *The Atlantic* magazine, wrote an article entitled "America Has No President: As the nation convulsed, the White House went dark." Literally. Supposedly.

Wrote Graham, "Last night, as protests convulsed Washington, D.C., the White House went dark. All the lights were off. The windows of the president's official residence were darkened, and the floodlights outside extinguished.

"The country is sick, angry, and divided, but it also finds itself leaderless. Trump has never shown any inclination or ability to soothe or console in moments of crisis. He wants the trappings of power, like showing up for a rocket launch, but he doesn't want to get his hands dirty with the work of governing. And he continues to view himself as the president only of the minority who voted for him, not all Americans. These tendencies have converged in this moment."

Whoa. Heavy.

There just one itsy bitsy potential problem with the visual aid Graham used as a metaphor to illustrate his point: the photo of the completely dark White House was quite possibly a photoshopped image of the White House from 2015 when President Obama and the First Lady Michelle were the residents.

Why did I suspect it could be phony? Well, the next day the "fact checkers" at the AP busted two individuals for using a bona fide fraudulent photo of the White House that looked exactly like the photo in Graham's story in *The Atlantic*. According to the AP, "The viral photo, which has been edited, can be found on Getty Image's stock website, where it was uploaded in December 2015. In the original, the lantern hanging in the White House portico is lit, along with several lights that surround the fountain in the front lawn. The edited version that is being widely shared online has been darkened and manipulated to remove the lit lantern."

I emailed Graham (his email is at the top of his article) and asked him about the photo. He responded saying "we have not used the same photo" as the one used by the two scammers busted by the AP. But because the photos appeared identical I immediately pressed him: was your photo a current shot of the White House? At the time of this post, I have not heard a reply to my second question from Graham. When and if he does, I will update this post. Until then, even though the photo used by ***The Atlantic*** appears identical to the busted photo, including the tell-tale darkened lantern, I must be charitable and assume, "if the photo don't fit, I must acquit." Ouch, bad analogy? Sue me. (Note: He never returned my email with the second question. Hmmm.)

So, who actually got publicly busted by AP for the fraud? The Digital Duo turned out to be none other than Democratic operative David Axelrod and former Secretary of State and 2016 Presidential Election Loser Hillary Rodham Clinton, who both used the phony image in separate June 2nd tweets for one purpose: to slam President Trump. I assume they were trying to "unite" the country. Ahem.

Axelrod called the "real" picture of a White House in the dark "perfect symbolism" for the Trump Presidency, while Hillary went whole hog. Her tweet contained side-by-side images of the old, photoshopped White House and the "fantastical" image of the White House when it was lit up with rainbow colors to celebrate the Supreme Court's decision to make gay marriage a constitutional right.

The words that accompanied the two photos in Hillary's tweet read: "Elections Matter."

Yes Hillary, I guess they do.

But then, WHAT DIFFERENCE, at this point, DOES IT MAKE???!!!!

EPILOGUE

Well, there you have it: 61 days of my reactions to the stupidity, hypocrisy and lies we all encountered during the horrible Coronavirus pandemic and the potential impact on the 2020 Presidential Election. I actually just the scratched surface as the amount of fodder thrown my way was ginormous.

If I could add one thing to this book, it would be the replies to my posts on Facebook from both supporters and detractors. The vast majority were supportive, with many simply hilarious. Others were downright mean, vile and profane enough to make Robert DeNiro and Alec Baldwin blush. Many of the latter were sent my way to make sure that I knew that I was a misogynistic, Islamophobic, homophobic bigoted, mouth-breathing and hate-filled moron. Oh, and, of course, a racist.

For the Liberals that read this book, they will find it maddening, but like most of the Liberals that replied to my posts, they will be long on name-calling, and short on countering the facts I have presented.

My guess is Conservatives will laugh, seethe, cheer and, hopefully, remember what they read when they enter a polling booth or put the stamp on their absentee ballot for the November election. Hopefully, they are playing by the rules and only sending in one ballot. Rest assured that some Democratic voters, some still dead, will pick up the slack and vote the "Chicago Way."

While I touched on the subject in this book, as I ended my writing, the whole notion of Liberal media censorship was just gaining steam and getting uglier by the day. Of course, much of that censorship is being targeted at Conservatives, most often President Trump. I expect this "free speech" war will only get nastier as we approach the election. Sadly, there is no middle ground. But then, in our hyper-partisan environment we find ourselves in, that notion is as passé as a guy holding open a door for a lady.

Don't get me wrong: Liberals promote "free speech" all day long, as long as your "speech" agrees with theirs. Otherwise you are a racist, bigot, oh hell, fill in the blank. In striking hypocrisy, it was the Liberals in this country that actually got the "Free Speech Movement" started in 1964 in Berkeley, California. Yeah, that same Berkeley where they destroy businesses and set stuff on fire whenever a Conservative speaker shows up on campus.

As I mentioned in my Introduction, if you like the book, share it with a friend, or better yet, tell them to buy a copy. If you hate it, put it in your bathroom knowing that all the "experts" are predicting a second round of the Coronavirus next year with another likely shortage of toilet paper. It may come in handy."

Finally, I will be voting in November for President Trump (provided he isn't assassinated by "comedian" Kathy Griffin) because, as Joe Biden so eloquently put it: "(I) ain't black".

ACKNOWLEDGMENTS

First and foremost, I want to thank my wife Betsy for putting up with me waking at 5 a.m. every morning to write what became of my daily Facebook posts contained in this book. However, I was not alone as I drank my coffee and composed because I had our trusty rescue pooch Sammy faithfully at my feet, patiently waiting for the Milk Bone treat I had hidden in my pocket.

A "bigly" thank you to genius, award-winning political cartoonist Henry Payne for the cover art and free usage of his previously published cartoons that grace the first page of each new chapter.

Thanks to my big brother Thom for providing occasional column ideas and his wise counsel on this book's Introduction. Also, thanks to my oldest son Zachary for demanding that I include Tiger King in the cover art. When I told him that Tiger King was not mentioned in any of my columns, he replied, emphatically, "So?"

A special thank you goes out to Speaker Nancy Pelosi, the Cuomo Brothers, "Comedian" Jimmy Kimmel, "Journalist" Chuck Todd, former VP Joe Biden, MSNBC, CNN, *The New York Times*, *The Washington Post*, Michigan Governor Gretchen "Almond Joy" Whitmer, the moronic gun-toting protesters in Michigan, Wacky Congresswoman Maxine Waters, the World Health Organization and a host of other politicians, celebrities and "journalists" who offered up what seemed like a 24-hour, all-you-can-eat buffet of stupidity, hypocrisy and lies during the months of April and May, 2020.

Thank you also to my many supporters on Facebook who constantly asked me if my columns would find their way into a book and a special thank you to the most vile, potty-mouthed and bitter Facebook "friend" who angrily told me to "get a job." Which I did: this book.

Finally, thank you to my publisher, Barbara Terry, and her gang of editors, layout experts and publicists -especially Baris Celik- for promising the manuscript delivered to them on June 1 would be released in September, two months ahead of the 2020 Presidential Election.

ABOUT THE AUTHOR

Jason Vines is a former long-time automotive executive and currently an author, lecturer, guest radio talk show host, and crisis PR consultant.

His first book, *"What Did Jesus Drive?: Crisis PR in Cars, Computers and Christianity"* won critical acclaim. The editor of *PR Week*, Steve Barrett, declared it "required read for all business school students." Democratic political strategist Joe Trippi said, "This is more than a corporate PR book - it's a masters' class, no holds barred, white knuckle ride of insights and wisdom for anyone whose job it is to communicate for a living."

Vines' second book, *"Jimmy Hoffa Called My Mom a Bitch: Profiles in Stupidity,"* is a compilation of his regular political satire columns from 2010 to 2014 on *The Michigan View*, the *Detroit News'* political website. The book quickly resulted in the Midwest's biggest radio station, WJR in Detroit, enlisting Vines as a morning guest host.

His third book, *"The Last American CEO,"* is the page-turning, behind-the-scenes story of Chrysler and its CEO Lee Iacocca's pursuit of American Motors Corporation and its prized position, the Jeep brand. It's the story of why Chrysler, now FiatChrysler, is alive today. The book, written side-by-side with the last CEO of American Motors, Joe Cappy, reads like a spy novel, but just happens to be all true.

Vines spent the vast majority of his career as an automotive executive, starting in labor economics and finally falling, by accident, into Public Relations. It worked out quite well for the skinny kid from the small Iowa town of Pella.

Vines was named the Top PR professional in the global automotive industry three times by the leading automotive industry magazine, *Automotive News*: once in 1999 for helping Nissan Motor Company regain its mojo while on the brink of bankruptcy and later, twice, in 2005 and 2006, leading the PR efforts to resuscitate the image of Chrysler Group, then a part of DaimlerChrysler.

Perhaps Vines' most famous, or infamous, work is his role two decades ago on the front lines for Ford Motor Company through the Ford-Firestone tire crisis, which began one week after Vines was named the head of Ford's global PR at the tender age of 40 years-plus-one-month. That work led to endless days and sleepless nights, a CBS' 60 Minutes investigation with Lesley Stahl and her producers up his keister for weeks, and three Congressional hearings; all with Vines' able hands in the open heart of the automaker leading the communications efforts and more.

Vines was "front page fired" for his efforts at Ford, along with his CEO Jacques Nasser. Bitter? Not Vines. As he was once told by a great friend, one he had to sadly fire: "Bitterness is a poison you take yourself."

Rather than bitterness, Vines decided to focus on being, as his wife says, "A complete smartass in his books. And, funnier than hell. I enjoy what he writes, unless it involves me." (NOTE: this last quote from Vines' wife was inserted due to a judge's settlement order. Oh, NOT! Just screwing with you!)

Throughout his career, in his books and continuing today, Vines has been a frequent college lecturer focusing on one, on-going theme: Why do we have such a hard time telling the truth? That theme pervades this book, and his previous publications, in spades, diamonds, clubs and hearts.

Vines resides in Mesa, Arizona with his wife of 34 years, Betsy. The couple have three adult children scattered around the country, and their best buddy, Sammy the Rescue Dog, who dutifully sat at Jason's feet almost every minute he wrote all four of his books, sometimes into the wee hours of the morning with lots of dog treats.

CPSIA information can be obtained
at www.ICGtesting.com
Printed in the USA
LVHW112246310820
664717LV00002B/452